Hello,
Gorgeous!

Blowout

Hello, Gorgeous!

Blowout

BY TAYLOR MORRIS

GROSSET & DUNLAP
An Imprint of Penguin Group (USA) Inc.

GROSSET & DUNLAP
Published by the Penguin Group
Penguin Group (USA) Inc., 375 Hudson Street,
New York, New York 10014, USA
Penguin Group (Canada), 90 Eglinton Avenue East, Suite 700,
Toronto, Ontario M4P 2Y3, Canada
(a division of Pearson Penguin Canada Inc.)
Penguin Books Ltd., 80 Strand, London WC2R 0RL, England
Penguin Group Ireland, 25 St. Stephen's Green, Dublin 2, Ireland
(a division of Penguin Books Ltd.)
Penguin Group (Australia), 250 Camberwell Road, Camberwell, Victoria
3124, Australia (a division of Pearson Australia Group Pty. Ltd.)
Penguin Books India Pvt. Ltd., 11 Community Centre,
Panchsheel Park, New Delhi—110 017, India
Penguin Group (NZ), 67 Apollo Drive, Rosedale, North Shore 0632, New
Zealand (a division of Pearson New Zealand Ltd.)
Penguin Books (South Africa) (Pty.) Ltd., 24 Sturdee Avenue,
Rosebank, Johannesburg 2196, South Africa

Penguin Books Ltd., Registered Offices:
80 Strand, London WC2R 0RL, England

Cover art by Anne Keenan Higgins

Library of Congress Control Number: 2010029885

ISBN 978-0-448-45526-6   10 9 8 7 6 5 4 3 2 1

To my gorgeous niece Haden, who inspires me more than she knows—TM

ACKNOWLEDGMENTS

I honestly can't thank the team at Grosset & Dunlap enough for their work on this book, especially Judy Goldschmidt. Thank you, Judy, for always being so patient with me and for not letting me get away with even one lazy sentence.

Major thanks also go to Micol Ostow, who not only tells me I have shiny hair, but who is responsible for leading me to this project. Thank you, Micol!

Thanks to Katie Carella, who always had great ideas and suggestions, and Bonnie Bader and Francesco Sedita, who started this whole thing in the first place. Thanks, everyone!

To my friend P.G. Kain—I can't thank you enough for your support throughout this whole process. Thanks for always being there for me with kind words and gossip.

Finally, thanks to my husband, Silas Huff, who has been so patient with me when I disappeared for days and weeks on end to write. You're the most supportive partner a girl could have!

—TM

CHAPTER 1

"Countdown to gorgeous!" cheered Megan as she passed me in the salon chair on her way to the back room. Megan, a college student with cascading blond hair and full, pink cheeks, was the receptionist at Hello, Gorgeous!, which happens to be my mom's salon and one of my very favorite places to be in the entire world. It was Sunday—my thirteenth birthday—and the salon wasn't open yet. Everyone was here special, just for me.

For as long as I can remember, my birthday presents have centered around hair. It started with my Barbie Princess Styling Head when I was four. I thought it was the greatest present ever invented. From the moment I got Barbie's head out of the box, I brushed, braided, curled, and clipped her hair within an inch of her princess-head life.

For my tenth birthday, my parents kicked it up a

notch when they surprised me with a smoky blue vanity desk with a three-way mirror. It came complete with matching containers filled with new brushes, combs, and clips. That's when I started styling my *own* head within an inch of its frizz-filled life. Still haven't had much luck there.

Last year, for my twelfth birthday, I got an actual styling chair for my bedroom, which gave my room more of a beauty-zone feel. It doesn't have the hydraulics to pump the seat up and down, but it's exactly like something you'd see in a real salon: black with a silver footrest and everything. I tried getting my best friend/next-door neighbor, Jonah, to sit in it so I could tame his cowlick, but he said he'd rather jam bobby pins up his nose than play hair salon with me.

But this year I finally received the best, most amazing birthday present ever. After a dinner at my favorite brick-oven pizza place last night with Mom and Dad, today I got my real birthday present—I became an official employee at Hello, Gorgeous!

Well, *part-time* (Saturday, Sunday, and Wednesday after school) official employee, but still. Mom had finally, after years of my begging, pleading, and tantrum-throwing, agreed to let me work as a sweeper at her über-successful salon. She was even going to pay me, though I totally would have done it for free. Mom went on and on about how it was a trial run and if I slacked off at the salon—or at school (Rockford Middle School)—I'd have to go. Which was never going to happen. I'd been waiting too long to be a part of the salon team, and the last thing I wanted to do was disappoint my mom. I wanted her to be proud of me and see that I had style-sense in my genes, too.

But my longing to work at Hello, Gorgeous! wasn't only about hair. I secretly hoped that working at a salon would give me some of the spark that all the stylists there seemed to have. You know, that sass that enabled them to say whatever was on their minds, in front of anyone, whenever it popped into their heads. I needed some of that. I'd been so painfully shy most of my life that I wouldn't even play Telephone with the kids in first grade. But unless I wanted Jonah to be my only friend for the rest of my life, I had to come out of my turtlelike shell. It was a must.

"How about some loose curls?" asked Violet. She was the store manager and most-talented stylist, and because of that she had the second-most prestigious station in the salon, second from the entrance, right beside my mother's. Not only was it my first day, but I was also getting a mini makeover as part of my birthday present.

When I came into Hello, Gorgeous! this morning with Mom, the salon had been dark and quiet until

I flipped on the light in the break room, where practically half the staff jumped up and yelled "Surprise!" I nearly fainted, but when I saw the doughnuts they'd bought and the two signs they'd hung—HAPPY BIRTHDAY, MICKEY! and WELCOME, GORGEOUS!—I knew it was going to be the most epic day of my life so far.

"My hair doesn't do curls," I said. It didn't wave or fall straight, either. All it ever did was frizz like the coat on a frightened billy goat.

"You don't even know the miracles Violet works with hair," Giancarlo said from the styling chair at his station, which was right next to Violet's. He swiveled back and forth, waving his checked crinkle scarf as he turned. He still had his sunglasses on because, in his words, "I'm getting blinded by my own shirt." The shirt in question was white silk with bright green, yellow, and pink swirls. "Just don't let her bump the top." A sly smile crept up on his round face. "Who wants to look like they've got a hamster hiding underneath their hair?"

"Give me a break," Violet said. She picked a round brush out of the drawer at her station and turned on the hair dryer to a low setting. Over the whizzing sound she said, "Just because I did it that one time!"

"One time too many!" Giancarlo said.

"Are you here to help?" Violet asked as she dried

my hair one section at a time. "Or are you just going to make fun?"

"Honey, I'm here to supervise." He did a full spin in the chair.

"Then why don't you try supervising Karen over there to do this girl's nails?" Violet pointed her chin to the back room, where Karen, who was tall and thin like a giraffe's neck, was leaning against the doorway. "And bring me another coffee from the back."

Giancarlo heaved his considerable weight up from the chair. "Only *you* can bring sanity to this place," he said to me, and walked toward the back where the break/supply room was. "Oh, Karen! You're needed!"

I loved the way they all bantered back and forth. Jonah and I had that, but otherwise I usually stayed pretty tight-lipped for fear of saying something stupid.

"So, Mick," Violet said to me as she expertly worked the round brush through my unruly hair. I was growing it long—it was all one length and almost halfway down my back—so there wasn't too much I ever did with it except pull it back in a ponytail. "You excited about your big first day?" Violet had an amazing pixie cut that looked like it was threaded with strands of gold, and today she was killing it in a one-shouldered, black jersey top with skinny black jeans and gold gladiators.

"I have butterflies," I confessed. "But the good kind. I think. I'm not nervous—I mean, I'm excited, but I hope I don't mess anything up. I mean, it's not like there's much to mess up since I'm just sweeping, but . . ."

"You'll be fine," she said, stopping my rambling. Even in front of people I'd known forever, I got nervous opening my mouth. "And don't fool yourself about just sweeping—every job counts because, honey, it takes a team to make women look as gorgeous as we do. Just make sure you sweep the stations clean before the clients arrive. Otherwise, we all look sloppy."

Karen came up from the back. "Since it's a special occasion and all, I'll do your nails right here in Violet's chair," she said.

I felt like Dorothy in *The Wizard of Oz* getting pampered and beautified at the palace salon in preparation for the most important moment of her life. "We need to get a move on," Karen continued. "Salon opens in thirty. What color did you decide on?"

"Um, there's one that's kind of mandarin orangeish? I saw it in the box of new spring colors in the back."

"Look at this one," Karen said to Violet, who just smiled as she worked on another section of my hair. "'The new spring colors.' She's sure not here to mess around."

"I think it'll look great with what I'm wearing.

Right?" I asked Violet. I had carefully planned my first-day outfit: a bubblegum pink T-shirt with a black silhouette of a girl wearing a high ponytail and fluffy bangs, a black, frayed denim skirt, and silver-sequined ballet flats.

"Absolutely," she nodded. "It'll look fantastic."

As Violet finished up my hair and Karen worked on my nails, Giancarlo came over with Megan, and they all gathered around me like I was Disney's newest It Girl. I loved every second of it. I'd been coming into the salon my whole life and had known most of them forever. They were always nice to me when I popped in with my dad or hung out with Mom after school, but this was different. This was me being a part of their world.

Violet turned off the hair dryer and gently brushed my long hair over my shoulders. "I didn't think you could get any prettier but . . . wow. You look stunning."

Just then, Mom walked onto the floor from her office. She stopped behind my chair and said, "Geez, Violet. This . . ." Mom fixed her green eyes on me. Her own black hair was smoothed back into a bun, and she looked chic as always in a black pencil skirt and crisp white button-down. She propped her fists on her hips and said, "This is beautiful. Nice work on these waves, Violet."

"You mean nice job smoothing out my frizz," I said.

"Your hair is not frizzy," Mom said.

Lie. Total lie. My hair *was* frizzy, and there didn't seem to be anything anyone could do about it. That was one reason why I was growing it out. The longer my hair was, the more its weight pulled out the frizz.

"You look," Mom said, "gorgeous."

"Ha, ha," I said. "I get it—*gorgeous* . . ."

"You are über-glam," Violet said. "Glamsational!" she said, pausing for effect. "Glamtastic!"

Mom patted my shoulder. "Ten to opening, everyone." She went to the computer at reception to check the day's schedule. I blew on my orange nails to help them dry faster.

The front door opened and a stylist walked in—the newest one, who Mom had just hired last week from Boston.

"Hi, Devon," Megan said with her signature perky voice.

"Hey," Devon said with a little less oomph than Megan.

As she headed for her station across from Violet's, I noticed Devon looked different from everyone else. Well, everyone at the salon looked different from regular people; it's like they shone brighter and buzzed with more energy. But Devon had a funky

16

look and mellow attitude all her own. Her hair was jet black with short, blunt bangs and was barely long enough to be pulled back into the tiny elastic that was holding it together in a ponytail. And she wore a black floral dress with combat boots and bright red matte lipstick.

I took one last look at myself. "Violet, thank you so much. I really love it," I said. "I just wish..." I stopped before I said anything else. I didn't want to sound stupid or ungrateful.

She cleaned and sterilized the brush and said, "Wish what? Spill it, sister."

"I just wish I could make my hair look like this every day. I could never fix it like this in a million years and, believe me, I've tried."

"I don't know what you normally look like," Devon said, walking over from her station. "But you look good today."

My face flushed at the new girl overhearing my confessions to Violet. "Thanks," I said.

"But you know what the first step is to being able to style your own hair to perfection?" Devon asked.

"What?"

"A good haircut." She reached out and felt the ends of my hair. I recoiled just a bit—something about the way she looked at my hair, like a scientist with her latest experiment, made me uncomfortable. "I could cut your hair. Something to help give you some bounce. And you'd look good with bangs."

Bangs? Not in a million, not with my wild hair. "I'm letting my hair grow out. And my mom cuts my hair."

She shrugged. "Just sayin'. I could do something amazing if you'd let me have at it."

She did a weird little finger-gun-shooting-at-me thing before going to her station.

I didn't want to break it to her, but the relationship between client and stylist was one of trust, and the fact was, I couldn't trust anyone who suggested I cut bangs.

"Doors opening!" Megan called from the front.

I rushed to the dressing room, ditched the super luxurious black, batiste cotton robe provided by the salon to protect the clients' clothes, and put my first-day shirt back on. My nails were still the tiniest bit tacky, so I had to be careful. I did a quick check of my hair (still perfect) and face (still . . . there) in the mirror. Then I grabbed a broom, scanned the room, and took in the last moments of quiet before the most important day of my life began.

I was ready.

CHAPTER 2

"Mickey, this floor isn't going to clean itself!"

"Mickey, watch your back!"

"Mickey, could you help me out here? Grab some fresh towels."

"Mickey, my station? My next client will be here any second!"

The quiet salon I had walked into had quickly given way to a clattering of noises—water splashing in sinks, heels clacking on floors, clients and stylists talking, and hair dryers blowing. Hair clipped with sharp scissors fluttered to the floor nonstop. The stylists asked me to do something for them every time I passed—get them more gel, bring them a clean towel, and, of course, sweep their stations. I worked as fast as I could to keep up even as little beads of sweat formed on my upper lip. I was trying as hard as I could, but I felt like I was slipping.

The front of the salon was just as busy as the floor, with women waiting patiently for their names to be called, flipping through magazines, sipping drinks, and chatting with one another.

"You're telling me you've lived in Rockford for ten years and you've never once visited us?" Megan said to a woman who had just been styled by Giancarlo. "I'm shocked. Shocked!" she said as the woman laughed.

"I won't make that mistake again," she said, fluffing up her lightened, brightened hair.

"Mickey?" Megan said when the woman headed out the door. "Could you please show Mrs. Klein to the back to get changed? Thanks," she said, before I could answer. After delivering the bobby pins, I was supposed to help Gladys—who had short, curly hair and helped with the cleaning—fold towels in the back, but I couldn't just leave Mrs. Klein hovering at the reception area. Turned out that being a sweeper wasn't exactly as limiting as I thought it'd be. I tried my hardest to keep up because the last thing I wanted was to see Mom's disappointed eyes turning on me.

"Um, hi," I said to Mrs. Klein, who had taut skin on her face and wrinkly skin on her neck. "Uh, right this way."

In my head, I had the most exciting personality. I was witty, charming, and made hilarious observations.

Out loud and in the real world, though, I was so generic I might as well have been a robot.

I tried to think of something funny and clever to say as Mrs. Klein and I walked through the salon. "You better not take so long between cuts this time," is what I came up with. I was trying to sound like Megan had with that last customer, but somehow I managed to sound just plain rude.

"Pardon me?" she said, turning her taut face to me.

"I just mean, uh—ha-ha! You know, six weeks between cuts, we want to make sure you stay looking gorgeous!"

Rowan, the esthetician, or skincare specialist, leaned in the doorway to the little room she worked in, her arms crossed. Her red hair was pulled back in a ponytail, bursting out in wavy curls from the black elastic. She raised an eyebrow at me as I walked past her with Mrs. Klein, and I knew she'd heard. I wasn't sure if I should have been upset for saying something dumb or happy that I'd said anything at all. I looked at Mrs. Klein, but I couldn't tell if she was angry at my stupid comment—the expression on her tight face changed so little.

"Right in here," I said, opening the changing room door and handing her a robe.

Hello, Gorgeous! sat on Camden Way, the most exclusive street in our town, between Esquire Cleaners and a bakery/coffee shop called CJ's Patisserie. The street has the best shops in town, like an actual cheese monger (which is a fancy name for expert), a high-end bakery that specializes in wedding cakes, and an old-fashioned shave shop, where men pay to get a straight-edged shave. And then there's Hello, Gorgeous!, home to the best stylists in all of New England, with the most famous, rich, and particular clients around. "Particular," by the way, is Mom's code for demanding.

After showing Mrs. Klein to the changing room, I headed back to help Gladys like I'd promised—only Giancarlo intercepted me before I could.

"Your presence is requested at reception, lovey," he said, his sunglasses now propped up on his bald head.

I took a quick look around the floor and realized that it was dusted with cut hair on both sides of the salon. I picked up the pace, hoping to help out Megan quickly so I could sweep up before Mom saw it.

Mom was working on a client at her station, which was right in the front, and I tried to dart past her. I didn't want her ever to have to tell me to do something at the salon—I'd vowed to myself that I'd be so on top of things that she'd never have to. When I looked at her to make sure she wasn't looking at me, she caught my eye and gave me a tight smile, which I knew was a bad sign.

"Where is your smock?" she asked in a low, but stern voice as I passed her.

"Oh. In the back. I'll get it."

"And the floors, Mickey," she said.

The dreaded smock! The sweepers and cleaners, like Gladys, had to wear those plastic monstrosities. I was hoping Mom would make an exception for me, but no dice.

Up front, Megan was on the phone and greeting clients at the same time, asking them to have a seat in the packed lounge area and offering them drinks while they waited.

"Hey, Mickster," she said when she saw me. "Could you get Angela there a bottle of water?" She pointed to a woman with pin-straight auburn hair and large sunglasses.

"Sure," I said. "Um, where can I find one of those smocks like Gladys's?"

"Oh, shoot!" she said, looking down at my outfit. "Yes, I totally forgot. Your mom will kill us both if she sees you without it. Salon rules. There should be some in the back room, in the cabinet next to the towels."

"Bring a diet soda, too!" Megan called. Like the batiste robes, drinks were another luxury Mom offered at the salon.

I got the smock, stopped off at the drinks station, which was right next to the manicure station, and then hustled back up front and handed the water to Angela.

"Thanks, girl. The diet is for Nicole." Megan pointed at Nicole, and I almost dropped the bottle when I realized who she was.

"Hello there, Mickey," Nicole, aka my homeroom teacher, Ms. Carter, said with a sly smile.

Oh my gosh. Awkward!

"Hi," I said, twisting the top off the soda bottle for her. I should have heard the sound before I felt the spray, but I was so distracted by Nicole (!) that I didn't realize the soda was fizzing all over my hand . . . the floor . . . and Ms. Carter's linen shorts, not to mention her legs.

"I'm so sorry!" I said, twisting the top back on and turning to look for a towel. I bumped right into Megan, who was already rushing over with paper towels she had pulled out ninja-style from underneath the counter.

"Here you go," she said, handing Ms. Carter the paper towels as she soaked up the rest on the floor. "You send us the dry cleaning bill for those shorts, okay?"

"I'm sure it'll be fine," she said, dabbing at her shorts and bare legs.

She may have said it was fine, but she had a look on her face that was more like the one she had when Andrew Zimmer brought a garden snake into class. I wanted to die. I knew I'd probably see kids from school at the salon, but for some reason it never, not in fourteen trillion years, occurred to me that *teachers* would come into the salon—without any makeup on and in regular, non-teacher clothes. The silk tank she wore showed off arms that were as ripped as Madonna's. She probably lived on a steady diet of protein shakes and bloody red meat. Maybe she even did bicep curls while grading our papers. *What if she's secretly one of those Las Vegas bodybuilders who gets all oiled up and flexes their quads in a bikini onstage?*

"I'm so sorry," I said again.

"Not to worry," she said tersely, like she was pretending (not very well) that she wasn't irritated. "I'm just a little sticky now." She snatched another paper towel from Megan.

"Mickey, get her some water," Megan said. My stomach dropped. I felt bad spilling the drink all over her, but hearing the flat tone in Megan's voice made me feel even worse. I had let her down.

"Sure," I said as tears tried to launch themselves out of my tear ducts. I forced them back. *Not today, ladies. Not today.*

Just as I got a bottle of water for Ms. Carter, I heard my name again.

"Mickey!" Devon snapped. "Could you *puh-leeze*?" She pointed to the floor of her station.

"Okay, sorry," I said, more worried about Mom catching me in the act of severe ineptitude than about Devon's voice. I grabbed my broom, which was leaning against the wall by the hair-washing sinks, and quickly swept Devon's station, scooping up hairs into the red dust pan.

Just as I was standing up from pushing every last hair onto the pan, Devon shooed me away—she actually shooed me! With a flick of her wrist she said, "Can't you go a bit quicker? Client coming. Oh, hi! Nice to meet you! I'm Devon."

Okay, don't get me wrong. I'm a girl who knows her place. I don't pretend like I'm something special just because my mom owns the joint. But this . . . *new chick* didn't have to treat me like I was her personal whipping girl.

Nobody shoos Mickey into the corner!

I felt my neck heating up with anger—at myself for not being quicker on the job, and at Devon for treating me like some nobody.

Understatement alert: The day was not going well. I was a terrible sweeper.

I tried to calm myself down in the back room.

Because if I didnt' pull myself together soon, my Hello, Gorgeous! career would be over before it ever began.

CHAPTER 3

There's a lot of talk in hair salons. Everyone knows that clients treat their stylists like therapists, telling them their deepest, darkest secrets. So just by being in the salon I overheard a lot of conversations.

Violet and Giancarlo talked about the arrival of Violet's mom and how Violet could get through the visit without going all Freddy Krueger on her.

"Send her to a show in Boston," said Violet's client, a woman in her early twenties who wore tortoiseshell glasses.

I even overheard Ms. Carter tell Karen that she had to go home and write a pop quiz for class tomorrow.

"Pop quizzes," Karen said as she brushed brick-red polish across Ms. Carter's nails. "I remember those."

After my disastrous morning, I was determined to keep my head down and concentrate on my work. But just as I started to think I was finally finding my groove, the chime above the door announced the arrival of two very special girls.

Lizbeth Ballinger and Kristen Campbell.

No, they were not celebrities of the movie, TV, or reality kind, but they were like the Demi and Selena of Rockford Middle School. Like, shut it down because these girls *owned* it. I'd seen them come into the salon before when I was just hanging out with my mom or Violet or Giancarlo. I always thought they were so much more sophisticated than I was because their hair and nails were perpetually done to perfection. Since, like, the fourth grade. I never really talked to them because it felt a little like they were out of my league.

I swept my mom's station as she took her client—Rosario Franco, who happened to be one of the local news anchors—up front to pay. Lizbeth and Kristen stood by the polish wall picking out colors for a manicure.

"I'm not loving any of these," Lizbeth said as she looked over all the colors.

"Not like you love *Matthew*, right?" Kristen laughed.

"Kristen, stop!" Lizbeth looked around to see if anyone heard and her eyes caught mine. The only Matthew I knew at school was a total prep named Matthew Anderson, whose mom was a Hello,

Gorgeous! client. Same Matthew? Probably. I quickly busied myself dusting Mom's station.

"Oh, I'm only kidding." Picking through the polishes, Kristen said, "I feel like I've worn them all before."

"Like, twice," Lizbeth said.

Mom came back and said to me, "Hey, honey. The drinks station is looking a little raggedy. Maybe you should straighten it up?"

"Sure," I said. The truth was, I was having a momentary panic. There was no way to get to the drinks station without Lizbeth and Kristen seeing me. In my smock. My *plastic* smock. Even though working at the salon was what I'd wanted more than anything in my whole life, suddenly how I looked to them—a smock-wearing weekend worker—made me hyperaware. Would they think I was kind of cool for having this job or kind of not?

As I arranged the drinks—sparkling water, regular, and three kinds of sodas, including extra cans of diet, the house favorite, Megan said, "Thanks, Mickey. Are you okay about the mess earlier?"

"Yes, I'm fine," I said quickly, trying not to draw too much attention to myself. I didn't want Lizbeth and Kristen seeing me in my smock *and* hearing I'd messed up *and* thinking that my working here was lame.

"You girls find colors you want?" she asked Lizbeth and Kristen.

"Not just yet," Lizbeth said, inspecting a bottle of teal that would look way too bright next to her ivory skin tone.

"Hey," Megan said, leaning against the counter and looking at them . . . and me. "I bet you girls all go to the same school, don't you?"

I actually felt my chest curving in and my shoulders hunching forward, as if I could make myself smaller and disappear from the scene. Lizbeth and Kristen turned their eyes toward me. They looked at me blankly as if I had just shown up at their party uninvited. With my parents. And a game of Candy Land tucked under my arm.

Okay. Even though we'd gone to the same school since kindergarten and had been in a couple of classes together over the years, it wasn't like we'd ever talked to one another. "Yeah," I finally managed, since they were still looking at me like I could infect them with my dullness. "We go to the same school."

"Um, yeah," Lizbeth said, looking unconvinced. She had dark brown hair, and her brown eyes seemed almost translucent. Especially when they were staring suspiciously at me. "You're in my history class, right?"

"No," I said. "But we had English together last year."

"We did?"

"Yeah."

See what I mean?

Once Megan had completed her task of creating a nightmare moment for me, she turned back to the front to greet a woman who was there to see Giancarlo. I went back to anonymity and straightened the drinks.

"I guess I'll just go with this one," Lizbeth said, taking the teal-colored polish back down from the shelf.

"I guess I'll go with my standard sheer pink," Kristen said. "Such a snore."

I hadn't planned to say anything, but I realized that I couldn't help myself. The teal was all wrong for Lizbeth and I happened to know that there was a great new color that would look perfect on her. It wasn't even in stores yet!

"Um. Hi. Again," I started. They looked at me like a fly they thought they'd waved out the window. "Well, it's just that, there are some new colors in the back that would look really good on you, Lizbeth. Also, I think there's something you'd like, too, if you wanted to try something new," I said to Kristen.

They looked at each other, and I prepared myself for them to push me away like Devon had. Instead, Lizbeth shrugged and said, "Yeah, sure."

"Okay, great," I said. I was happy to help and,

honestly, to actually be talking to them. But at the same time I worried whether they'd even like what I brought them. "Be right back."

In the back, I opened the box with the new shipment of spring colors, where I'd seen my mandarin orange polish. For a few weeks at the beginning of each season, the new colors were hugely in demand. We got a couple of bottles of each, and we reordered whichever ones were popular. I grabbed the two shades, one each for Lizbeth and Kristen, and hoped my color instincts were right. I took them to the front and showed them to the girls.

"This one is called Peppermint Shake," I said of the light green color with tiny pink sparkles. Lizbeth took the bottle and inspected it. "It'll look good on you. And this is called Cornflower Blues," I said, handing over a bottle of light blue polish to Kristen.

"*Love*," Kristen said of the polish.

"Yeah, seriously," Lizbeth said. "I haven't even seen these colors, like, anywhere."

"They're new for the spring season," I said.

Then I suddenly became hyperaware that I was talking to Lizbeth and Kristen and I froze. I stood there like a spaz and nodded my head.

"Well, thanks a lot," Lizbeth said. As I picked up my broom and started sweeping again, Lizbeth said, "And I like your hair."

I touched the ends with my free hand and said, "Violet did it."

Lizbeth smiled and said, "It looks good."

Just as I thought of something to say, Devon's voice cut through the salon.

"Mickey! My station!"

And whatever nugget of genius I had finally come up with fell right out of my head.

CHAPTER 4

I was so exhausted by the time I had my lunch, I felt like crumbling to the ground. I also felt defeated. Not soul-crushingly defeated, but not too far off, either. I mean, it's not like I expected to become some hair style maven in one day flat, but I had totally crashed and burned on the salon floor. Not long after lunch, Mom told me that maybe I'd had enough for my first day and said I could leave early.

My stomach sank, knowing I'd let her down.

When I got home, Dad was sitting on the couch, leafing through a cookbook.

"Hey, superstar," he said. "How was your first day?"

I dropped my bag by the couch and dragged my feet toward the kitchen.

"What's wrong? You didn't chop off someone's hair, did you?"

I took a Double Fudge Yoo-hoo out of the fridge and made my way back through the living room toward the stairs. "No. I'm just really tired."

"Well, wake up. I'm grilling shrimp for dinner!"

That was usually the one dish that could cheer me up after a bad day. *Usually.*

Upstairs in my room I grabbed a stack of magazines from my desk and dumped them on the floor by my bed. I sat cross-legged in front of them, sighed deeply, then picked up *Medusa*, one of my favorites that featured far-out looks that no one would ever wear unless they were walking down a Paris runway. I loved fantasizing about how I might one day be like Mom or Violet and have the most stylin' clients in town. Today, though, I saw those looks as a symbol of my failure—because how could I be a great stylist if I couldn't even do simple tasks like open a bottle of soda without creating a mess?

I had to remind myself that there was one good thing that had happened. I had actually spoken more than two words to Lizbeth and Kristen and didn't humiliate myself. I tried to take comfort in that, but knowing I still had to face Mom set my stomach in tight knots. She wouldn't care that I had spoken to some popular girls. All she'd care about was the fact that Devon had asked me to sweep her station twice.

When I heard Mom come home, I stayed hidden in my room. Why rush the inevitable? I didn't leave until Dad finally shouted for me to come down because my dinner was getting cold.

Dad brought out a plate of grilled shrimp with lemon and salad with cherry tomatoes and crumbled goat cheese. He knew this was one of my favorite spring dishes of his, and I felt a little guilty knowing he probably made it special for my big day.

Mom gave me a weak smile when she sat down. Even after ten hours on her feet, she still looked beautiful. Her hair had come a bit undone from her bun, but on her it looked like it was supposed to be that way.

When she sat down she placed her napkin in her lap and Dad served her shrimp and salad. I looked at my plate, wondering how I could possibly eat.

"Well, Mikaela," Mom began. I cringed hearing her use my full name. "How do you think today went?"

I pushed a shrimp across my plate. "Okay. I mean, it could have gone better."

"Okay, but it *was* your first day, sweetie. Don't look so defeated. Think about how you'll do better next time," she said as she speared a cherry tomato.

Total relief. I really thought she might rip my head off. After all, Mom didn't get to where she was by tolerating anything short of perfection.

"I'll pay better attention. Work faster." Not spill sticky drinks on teachers' legs. Avoid making nice stylists snap at me. Avoid certain stylists altogether . . .

She nodded and said, "That's the attitude!" before taking a bite from her shrimp.

I was all worked up over nothing, it seemed. But then, just as I was about to dig into a nice piece of shrimp myself, I felt her looking at me as if she had something to add.

"Honey, I know you were excited about your first day—"

Here we go . . .

"—and it was a lot to take in and learn. Just remember what your main job is, okay? Devon said she had to ask you twice to sweep up her station."

Unbelievable! Devon ratted me out on my first day!

I slumped in my seat. All of my excitement over starting at the salon was now replaced by disappointment. I figured keeping my mouth shut and proving my mom wrong when I worked on Wednesday was the best thing to do.

Later, I was over at Jonah's, and I was anxious to tell him how horribly things had gone. The Goldmans live right behind us and our dads are BFFs. They even built a gate in the fence that separates our backyards so they could go back and forth more easily.

"Here, this is for you," he said, before I could say anything. "Happy birthday." He shoved a long tin box into my hands. It was chipped yellow and had a little illustration of a girl brushing her hair on the cover.

"What is this?" I asked.

"An old pencil box. I got it at that junk store on Camden Way."

"Loretta's Treasures?" I asked. He nodded. Loretta's was a really nice antique store that had been on some PBS program once because of its rare toy collection.

"My mom was there buying some table thing and I saw it. I figured you could put, like, those little black things in it for your hair."

"Bobby pins?" I asked, knowing full well he knew what they were called but simply didn't want to admit it.

"Whatever." He shrugged. "Or clips or, I don't know. Whatever. Sorry I didn't wrap it."

"This is really cool, Jonah," I said, opening the lid. It was a little dusty inside, but it would go perfectly on my vanity set. And it really was the perfect size for bobby pins and small clips and hair bands. Score one for Jonah.

He started up Warpath of Doom, which I loved

because I usually whooped his you-know-what when we played. I'd held the record for three months straight, and today, while I was slaving away, he'd taken away my record. I couldn't change what had happened at the salon, but I could get that record back and set one thing right in the universe.

When I told him how horribly my day went, he responded by saying, "I bet it wasn't that bad." That's what you get when your only friend is a boy.

"Yeah, well, what do *you* know?" I said. "You don't have a job."

"Why would I want a *job*?" He said the word *job* like he would say the word *dolls* when we were kids. As in, "I'm not playing with your stupid *dolls*." "My job is to skateboard, play video games, and annoy you."

"Glad to see you've been promoted to full time."

"I have," Jonah said. "In fact, I'm thinking of getting my PhD in it, 'cause that's how awesome I am."

I stifled a smile and said, "I'm sure you've made your mother proud."

The game started up, and we jerked the controls through the first level. We both could have done level one in our sleep. "Did I tell you who came into the salon?"

"Who?" He shot down a bomber.

"Nicole Carter."

"Who's that?"

"*Ms.* Carter, my homeroom teacher, your history teacher?" I said.

"No way! What's she like on weekends? Wait, I'm not sure I want to know."

I smiled, snapping and pounding my controller to make sure I downed more enemy aircraft than he did. "And you'll never believe what I did. I let a bottle of diet soda explode all over her."

"Nice!" he said as he blew out an enemy bomb shelter. "At least it wasn't someone like Coach Petragallo. He would have made you run suicides or something. Ms. Carter is pretty cool."

"Yeah, well, she's giving you a pop quiz on Monday. How cool is that?"

Jonah almost stopped playing. "Seriously?"

I nodded. "Heard her say it."

He refocused his attention on the game. "Good to know."

"I hear all sorts of things there," I said, realizing just how much it was true.

"Yeah, well, if any more teachers come in announcing pop quizzes, let me know. Let the whole school know and you'll be everyone's new best friend."

I thought about that as I surpassed my all-time high score. What Jonah lacked in his ability to destroy even the smallest of tanks, he made up for with his (sometimes) clever ideas.

I didn't want to be *everyone's* best friend, but I definitely had room for a few more friends in my life, to say the least.

CHAPTER 5

"Good morning, Mickey," Ms. Carter said to me when I came to class on Monday. Even though she was back in her teacher clothes—makeup on, arms and legs covered, and her new brick-red nails shining—I couldn't get that bodybuilder image out of my head. I wondered if she'd had a glass of raw eggs for breakfast. "I hope you didn't work too much this weekend." She grinned like we shared a secret.

I glanced around the room to see if anyone had heard her. I was probably the only kid in school with a j-o-b, which made me suddenly feel way more mature than the other kids. Like, totally.

But, of course, no one even noticed Ms. Carter talking to me.

Later in the day as I walked down the hall, Jonah yelled my name as if I was about to open a door that had a fire blazing on the other side.

"Wait up!" he called. He was walking with his friend Kyle, who he sometimes skated with on weekends. "We have something *very important* to tell you."

"Oh yeah? What?" I said.

Jonah smacked Kyle in the chest with the back of his hand. "Tell her, man."

"Tell me what?" I asked.

"Uh, thanks," Kyle said.

Kyle, for all of you wondering, has the greatest hair. Big, beautiful curls. I didn't want to be envious of those curls, but I was. Oh, how I was. As for Kyle himself, he was . . . okay, if you liked people who spoke in half sentences, at best. Wait—I guess that's me most of the time. Well . . . at times I'm not so crazy about myself, either.

"Yeah, Mick," Jonah said. "Thanks for the heads up on the test in Ms. Carter's."

"Oh," I said. "You're welcome."

After Jonah and Kyle headed off to class, I made a quick stop in the bathroom. Lizbeth and Kristen were standing at the putty-colored sinks applying lip gloss and hairspray. I stopped cold and almost turned and stepped right back out the door. I wasn't sure why, exactly. I guess I didn't know if they'd talked to me yesterday at the salon because I was the help or because we were all in the same grade at the same school and I might be someone they'd consider hanging out with someday.

But I didn't want to be a complete wimp and run away from them. I had just as much right to be there as they did. Maybe they'd even talk to me or maybe a miracle would happen and I'd open my mouth and talk to them.

"I'm just saying, it was kind of weird, that's all," Lizbeth said to Kristen.

"What's the big deal? I was just being friendly."

"I don't care," Lizbeth said. "I was just saying it was weird how you were suddenly all over him the moment I pointed him out."

"Please, Lizzie. Not true," Kristen said.

"Can we just drop it? It's so not a big deal."

Kristen shrugged. "Dropped."

I stood in front of a mirror two down from them. *Tra la la.* I tried to look like I didn't have a single care in the world. *Was the him they were talking about related to the Matthew comment Kristen made at the salon?* I wondered. But really, the biggest question running through my mind was whether I should say hello first, or if I should wait and see if they might say something to me.

Should have known. Option C: They didn't even notice my existence. Just kept right on talking.

"You're coming over after school, right?" Lizbeth asked Kristen.

"After ballet," Kristen said. She made a little gagging noise.

I watched as Lizbeth brushed her shiny hair. She always looked like she'd just stepped out of Violet's chair, perfectly styled. I wondered how she did it on her own. I could style a doll's hair to perfection, no problem. But my own? If I wanted to look like I'd just been electrocuted, then yeah, I was great at doing my own hair.

"Do you want to borrow my camera?"

I was looking at Lizbeth in the mirror, and it took me a moment to realize that Kristen was talking to me. She held out her cell toward me, eyeing my reflection in the mirror. "So you can take a picture— it'll last longer."

"God, Kristen," Lizbeth said, looking embarrassed. I looked down at my bag, wishing I could crawl into it, zip myself up, and wait for them to leave. Lizbeth gave me an apologetic smile. "Sorry, Mickey."

"It's okay," I muttered.

"You're so rude," Lizbeth said in a low voice to Kristen.

"I was just joking. Sorry," she said to Lizbeth.

I couldn't explain why, but I wanted them to like me. Well, right then maybe not Kristen, especially since she thought Lizbeth was more deserving of an apology from her than I was. But more than wanting anyone to like me, though, I didn't want to be intimidated by them. I didn't want to be intimidated by *anyone*.

"I was just trying to remember," I said, in effort to cover. "Don't you have Ms. Carter for history?" I had no idea if they did, but it seemed like a good comeback after getting busted for staring.

Lizbeth said, "Yeah. Why?"

Whoa. Ten points for random guessing. "Have you had her class yet today?"

"No," Kristen said. "Why?"

I could feel my face burn with embarrassment. What was I doing? I was acting like we were all friends just chatting away in the bathroom when in reality they barely recognized me. From *yesterday*. I hadn't felt humiliation this deep since Andrew Zimmer yelled "Jonah loves Mickey!" during an assembly in first grade. Into a microphone! "Well, you know how I was working at Hello, Gorgeous! like, yesterday?"

Kristen stared back at me, her long, auburn hair laying across her shoulders with delicate comma curls at the ends. It was Lizbeth who spoke up and said, "Yeah, of course." She held up her Peppermint Shake nails. "I've already gotten two compliments today."

"Oh, cool," I said. "Well, um. See, Ms. Carter was in yesterday, too. I heard her say she was giving a pop quiz today."

"A pop quiz?" Kristen asked. "Are you sure?"

"That's what she said," I said.

Kristen nudged Lizbeth. "Great. I'm totally going to fail."

"No you're not. We'll study at lunch," Lizbeth said. She turned to me, "You are *such* a lifesaver. Thanks a lot."

I smiled. "Good luck."

"Come on, we gotta go," Kristen said to Lizbeth. Just before they left, Kristen turned back to me and said, "Hey, do you get free stuff at the salon? Because I love this nail polish you recommended." She showed me her Cornflower Blues. "But I feel like at any moment it's going to chip along the ridge of my nail."

"Oh yeah," Lizbeth said, examining her Peppermint Shake. "Me too."

I knew it was solid nail polish—we didn't use flaky stuff—but the truth was we did have a couple of bottles of each new color. Violet had probably already taken inventory of the extra bottles and stored them on the shelves, leaving the bottles the girls had used at Karen's manicure station.

"Yeah," I said. "I kind of get free stuff."

"Do you think you could get me a bottle for touch-ups?"

"Yeah, sure," I heard myself saying. I was pretty sure that Mom didn't want me giving stuff away, but maybe just this once—as long as it didn't become a habit. And it was pretty safe to assume no one would miss these colors too much—most of the salon clientele were chic adult-type women who would never be caught dead with mint-green or cornflower-blue nails. "I'll bring you some later this week. I don't work again until Wednesday. Is that okay?"

"Awesome," Kristen said. "Thanks!"

"See ya later," Lizbeth said as they left.

I stood staring at the door after it'd shut. Lizbeth and Kristen were grateful to me. I felt amazing—the salon was already working its magic on me, transforming me into someone who talked to people—*popular people, even!*

Now all I had to do was not blow it—which for me was not as easy as it seemed.

CHAPTER 6

On Wednesday morning, I put on a black-and-white striped T-shirt over leggings with a gray self-belting cardigan and lace-up booties and planned to fully redeem myself at the salon later that day. I went through my normal styling routine of washing, conditioning, and applying defrizz balm. Then I set the hair dryer on low and used the round brush to work my hair into big, gentle curls like Violet had done. Unfortunately, the round brush was my kryptonite. (Notice the words you learn having a *boy* for a best friend.) I was determined to master it one day, but today wasn't that day. Also, Mom was yelling for me to hurry up, so I had to bail. I cranked up the power on the blow-dryer and blasted my hair. And then, like most other days, I pulled it back into a fuzz ball ponytail.

When I got to the salon after school that day, I

snapped on my smock, then grabbed my broom and gripped it tightly in my hands as if it were an extension of my body. I was determined not to let go of it all day.

Wednesday evening may not have been as busy as Sunday, but that didn't mean it wasn't crazy. Violet was still working a packed schedule when I got there. Rowan had facials lined up till closing. Piper, a college-age strawberry blonde, was on shift and so was Devon. The smell of product wafted around me, a combination of sweet and chemical, and the warm lights gave a sense of serenity to a place that was otherwise a whirlwind of activity.

In my mind, I was calm and competent, a true professional; on the floor, however, sweat still beaded on my upper lip as I did an Olympic speed-walk from the back of the salon to the front, carrying fresh cotton balls and extra buffing blocks for Karen's manicure station.

I kept such an eagle eye out that I noticed every dust mite drifting through the air. I was so concerned about keeping Devon's station clean that I practically held the dust pan under her poor clients' heads as she clipped. "Uh, yeah, thanks," Devon said. Today she wore cuffed dark denim jeans with a form-fitting plaid shirt and Doc Martens. "But could you please hold off until we're done here?"

"Sorry," I muttered. I hated to admit she was right, but she was. I wasn't supposed to sweep when clients were sitting in the chair. I just got a little carried away with myself.

I moved over to Violet's station just seconds after she was done with her client. My timing was perfect and I managed to pick up every speck of dust. Then, just as I was congratulating myself for perfecting my technique, my foot caught the edge of Devon's styling trolley. Time stood still for exactly one second and then, chaos. I flew forward and landed with a giant *thud* on my knees. Next, I heard the scattering and clattering of style supplies on the shiny marble floor. Devon's trolley had come down with me, blowing the entirety of its contents of brushes, butterfly clips, and hundreds of tiny bobby pins all around me. I slowly regained my balance and got back up on my feet, only to slip again, calling everyone's attention to the disaster I had caused.

"Mickey! Are you okay?" Violet asked, rushing over. Everyone looked at me like the train wreck that I was.

I stood up as quickly as I'd gone down, trying to act like it was just a little tumble. My knee throbbed, but I tried to play it off. Devon had already started picking up her loot, but not before she shot me a look and apologized to her client.

"Well," I said to Violet but loud enough for the others to hear, "it was a great trip. I'll see you next fall!" I tried not to limp to the back, but when I got to the break room I rubbed my knees as tears popped out of my eyes like tiny little geysers. I couldn't have held them back if I wanted to.

"Honey, what happened?"

I looked up from rubbing my knees and saw through watery eyes Mom standing in the doorway. Had that been so loud that she heard it from her office? And then I realized I hadn't even stopped to help Devon clean up the mess I'd made. Great. Another reason for her to hate me.

I kept my back to Mom as I quickly wiped the tears from my face. "Nothing. Just a little spill," I said, trying to steady my voice. "I'm cleaning it up right now."

I got up to go back out and face the floor, but Mom stopped me, putting her hand on my shoulder. She gave my cheek a little pat. "You'll pull through it," she said. I wasn't so sure, but I left the back room with my head held high.

I tried to help Devon finish cleaning, but she snapped under her breath, "I'd just organized this." She then seemed to remember that I was an actual human because she said, "You okay?"

I quickly nodded yes and squeaked out an apology. Anything more and I was sure I'd start boo-hooing like a baby.

"Mickey," Violet called from her station. "Come here for a sec." I'm sure she was just trying to get me out of the spotlight and away from Devon's menacing eyes.

Violet stood behind Alicia, who I knew was a longtime client. Her hair was down to the middle of her back, thick with tight curls. "You want to get me one of those new headbands from up front for Alicia? Maybe the one with the peacock feathers?"

"Sure," I said. Even though I'd told myself I would only concentrate on sweeping, I couldn't exactly say no when a stylist asked me to help with something.

I went to the accessories counter by reception.

"I need to get something for Violet," I said to Megan, pointing to the glass case that held the hair accessories we sold.

"Sure," Megan said. She smelled like green apples and had a big, red flower clipped on the side of her blond hair. "Key is by the fish bowl."

When she said fish bowl, she meant the big glass bowl into which people dropped their business cards and contact information for the drawings we did randomly. And when I say randomly, I *mean* randomly. Like whenever we felt like it. Giancarlo had a calzone for lunch? Time to draw. Violet has a hangnail? Better draw! Megan's wearing blue today? Sounds like it's time to draw! The prizes were free treatments like facials, massages, and manicures.

I grabbed the key and unlocked the accessories counter. Mom and Megan picked out goodies from a catalog of stuff we got from a supplier, and sometimes they bought stuff made by locals in the Berkshires. Those were usually my favorites, unique to our little section of the world. I thought it was pretty cool having something that glamorous people in big cities like New York or even Los Angeles didn't have.

I took out the peacock-feathered headband Violet asked for but glanced back to get another look at Alicia's dark hair. The rich, deep colors of the headband would get lost in her color and I worried that the headband wouldn't have the strength to hold back her thick hair. So I also chose a vibrant blue flower clip made from metal that reminded me of the Cornflower Blues nail polish I'd recommended to Kristen. I figured Alicia's hair would actually benefit from the heavy weight of the clip.

I brought them both over to Violet and said, "The headband is nice, but I was thinking this clip could work really well."

She held it up to Alicia's hair and said, "You're right, this works so much better. Really brings out your eyes, Alicia."

"Yeah, I love it. It's really pretty."

I tried to play it cool—*Yeah, no biggie, I always choose killer accessories for clients*—but the truth was I was bursting with joy. I started to tell Alicia about the Cornflower Blues nail polish in case she wanted to get a manicure to match the new clip, but she and Violet had gone back to talking and besides, it really wasn't my place to butt in. After my spectacular display of grace when I'd tackled Devon's cart, I figured my best bet was to keep my trap shut and my broom moving. And move it I did—in a wide circle around Devon's station as she worked on the client.

Still, it was like she wanted to punish me for disrupting the perfect order of her little trolley cart thing. "Hey," she called to me as she sheared the woman's long red hair. "Bring me a water, will you?"

What I wanted to say was, *"Pardon?"* A little *please* and *thank you* wouldn't have killed her.

I grabbed a bottle of water from the drinks station and when I brought it to her she was laughing her head off. Probably talking about my fall.

"She must have been freaking out," the woman laughed. *(About my fall?)*

"She was *speechless*," Devon said. (No, I *wasn't*!)

"Here's your water," I said, holding the bottle out to her and being all, *I'm standing right here so you can quit talking about me!*

She ignored me, so I placed the bottle on her counter and walked away, intent on sweeping under the accessories counter before she could ask me to do something else.

Still laughing, Devon lowered her voice and said, "It's not every day I make a girl go bald!" Then she and her client started giggling again.

Say wha . . . ? I almost tripped over my broom. I couldn't believe it.

Look, I'm no snitch, but for a moment I seriously thought about marching right back to Mom's office and telling her. Devon must have given some poor woman such a bad haircut that the only solution was to shave her head. My brain didn't even know where to start. How could Mom have hired her if she was a menace to all heads of hair? It was like hiring a thief to work in a bank.

It's not like I needed an excuse, but now there was no way I'd ever let her get near me with a pair of scissors. I'd let Jonah cut my hair before her. I'd get myself *fired* before I ever let her come near me—that's how dead set I was on never, not in a million years, letting Devon within four feet of my head with a pair of scissors. EVER.

CHAPTER 7

At the end of the day, as I was getting my bag to head home, I spotted the bottles of spring nail polishes, now neatly lined up on the storage shelf—including Peppermint Shake and Cornflower Blues. I had kind of already promised them to Lizbeth and Kristen, but after the day I'd had, there was no way I could have asked my mother to let me just have them.

I couldn't stand the thought of showing up to school empty-handed on Thursday. And like I said, those two colors weren't likely to be missed. So I decided to take them. I snatched the two bottles and dropped them in my bag and, just like that, the deed was done.

As I left the back room I almost bumped into Rowan as she came out of the small, private treatment room. She startled me so much, it's a miracle I didn't drop my bag. Can you imagine how awful that would have been?! The bottles spilling out onto the floor, Rowan catching me red-handed and telling on me to Mom, who would have grounded me for life?!

"Easy, girl," Rowan said, her kelly green eyes looking down at me suspiciously. Okay, maybe not, but that's how it felt. I wondered if I shouldn't sneak them back onto the shelves ("Why, how did *these* get in my bag?") but instead I hustled out the door and headed home.

The next day at school I kept an eye out for Lizbeth and Kristen, feeling a twinge of guilt for taking the polishes.

I didn't have any classes with them, so I had to be a bit stalkerish looking for them in the halls. I also checked the bathroom before and after every class. (I will only admit to this being *borderline* pathetic.) By the time lunch rolled around and I still hadn't seen them, I decided to hang around outside the cafeteria hoping to casually bump into them. Easy.

"Waiting for me?" Jonah asked as I leaned against the wall. Kyle was with him, his hair hanging down over his eyes.

"How'd you know?" I said. "And now that you're here, go fetch me my lunch and warm up my seat." Kyle was once again staring at his shoes. "Hey, Kyle. What's up?"

He muttered in response.

"You coming over tonight?" Jonah asked. "I got this killer new game with these amazing new graphics . . ."

Just then, I saw Lizbeth's honey blond hair bobbing down the hall toward us. Finally!

"Yeah, yeah, yeah," I said to Jonah, trying to nudge him into the cafeteria so that I could have some time of my own with Lizbeth and Kristen.

"This new game has, like, orbit levels and aliens, but not the stupid kind that are totally lame. Hey, why are you shoving me?"

"Those orbits sound amazing. Totally. So, yeah! We'll see the aliens tonight, okay?"

"What's your problem?" Jonah asked.

"Great! Aliens it is!" He looked at me like I'd suddenly sprouted antennae. "Sorry, I mean I'll meet you inside, probably," I finished, because maybe I'd end up sitting with the girls. "Bye!"

"You are so weird and annoying sometimes," he said, and he and Kyle finally left me alone.

I panicked as Lizbeth and Kristen got closer. How should I approach them? Would they think I was totally weird? Would they know I was stalking them? Wait, no, I was *not* stalking them. Just looking for them. Totally different.

I stood in their way like a support beam and they practically slammed right into me.

"Oh, sorry," I said.

"No probs," Kristen said. She had on the most adorable blue, teal, and white sundress.

"Hey, Mickey," said Lizbeth.

"Hey," I said. "Hi."

They continued walking. My mind went blank. I stood immobile, watching the moment pass me by. Why couldn't I speak up? Why couldn't I say anything? Why was I so—

"Wait!"

Smooth, Mick. Real smooth.

They turned back to look at me. Kristen crinkled her brow. I thrust the polish bottles toward them. "Here. These are for you." They both stepped forward, looking at my outstretched hand as if I were holding a poison dart frog, which of course would leap and attack them at any moment. (Familiarity with amphibious life, courtesy of one Jonah Goldman.)

"Oh," Lizbeth said when she saw it. "Our polish. Cool."

"Awesome, thanks," Kristen said.

"You're welcome," I said as they both took a bottle. Then, before I realized what was happening, Lizbeth was saying "See ya," and I was watching them walk into the cafeteria. Without me. Clutching bottles of nail polish. Bottles that I had *stolen* just for them.

Now I could admit to full-on pathetic-dom.

I sighed and went to sit with Jonah and Kyle. "Glad you could join us," Jonah said when I asked him to scootch down to make room for me. "Now you can be our judge: Who has the biggest bicep?" I sighed as they flexed their sad, little muscles, realizing I might be forever exiled to the sad land of boydom.

Why was I *such* an idiot? There was nothing about Lizbeth and Kristen that was so special I couldn't approach them. It's not like they were starring in their own vampire movie with the planet's hottest leading guy or anything. They were regular people, just like me, so what was there to be nervous about?

I found myself thinking of Giancarlo. He'd probably say something like, "Honey, who are *they*? Those girls should be intimidated by you."

So I went back to my stalker ways and kept an eye out for them after school. I was standing in the foyer, digging through my bag and folders, doing anything to look like I was doing *something*, when Lizbeth turned the corner toward the front doors of the school.

"Oh!" she said just before our foreheads met like rams in a fight.

"Ow!" I said as bright stars swirled in the space between us. "Are you okay?"

"Yeah." Lizbeth laughed, rubbing her head. "I don't really use this much, anyway. Are you okay?"

"I think so." I said. We stood for a moment kind of

laughing and rubbing our heads. I knew that if I didn't start a conversation then, I'd be angry with myself for days.

"Speaking of heads," I began. Lame, but I forged ahead. "How'd that quiz go? In Ms. Carter's class?"

Lizbeth stopped rubbing her head, then said, "Oh my gosh. The quiz. I am so rude. I never thanked you a million times for telling us about that. I got an A."

"Awesome," I said, feeling amazing. We started out the front doors and down the steps.

"Do *many* of the teachers come into your salon?" Lizbeth asked.

"She's the only one I've seen." I had a thought—a risk I wanted to take. I said it before I gave myself any time to think about it. "Lots of kids' parents, too. You know, like"—I lowered my voice—"Matthew Anderson's mom."

Lizbeth's eyes darted toward me. I held my breath. "I had a feeling you might have overheard us that day Kristen and I were there getting manicures." She sounded grateful for the chance to talk about him, which was a huge relief. A comment like that could have landed different ways. Lizbeth could have been mad that I was butting in.

"He's cute. I mean, *I* don't like him," I added because I didn't want her to think I was going after her man or anything. He *was* cute, though, if you liked the preppy kind. I don't think he'd been seen in a shirt without an alligator on it since he left the hospital after his mother gave birth to him. "Just so you know . . ."

Lizbeth nodded her head slowly. "He *is* cute. Just please don't tell anyone, okay? Kristen loves to tease me about it just to see how far she can go. It makes me nervous. He doesn't know I like him and, well, I'm not ready yet for him to know."

"Don't worry. Secret's safe." I mimed locking my lips.

She smiled. "So with that and Ms. Carter's quiz, you must hear tons of good stuff at the salon, huh?"

"Yeah, I hear stuff."

"Anything juicy?" Lizbeth asked. Her amber eyes lit up, like she really wanted to hear some good dirt.

"Well," I said, trying to think. I didn't want to let her down. She obviously appreciated the quiz notice, but didn't seem to care about the nail polish. And now that she'd confessed her secret love, I felt like I had to give her something good, too. I didn't have much to offer, though. Except, well, there was that one thing. "We have this new stylist at the salon, Devon. And, um, I heard her telling this one customer that at her old salon she accidentally made a client of hers go bald."

"No way!" Lizbeth cheered.

"Totally," I said. "It's probably why she had to leave Boston and move here. Maybe she was run out of town or something."

"Making someone go bald. Wow, I can't imagine," Lizbeth said, shaking her head. "Her name's Devon?"

I nodded.

"I'm staying away from her, that's for sure."

"Me too," I said. "And wouldn't ya know—she's trying to get me to let her cut my hair! It's getting to a point where I almost have to duck every time I see her!"

And there it was—a whole conversation with Lizbeth Ballinger. Friday night slumber parties and family vacations couldn't be far behind!

Just as I was worrying about what to say next, Kristen came over and joined us, and Lizbeth's mom pulled up in her car. I was saved. "Hey, guys," said Kristen, tucking a strand of hair behind her ear. "What are you talking about?"

"I'll tell you on the ride home. It's a good one," said Lizbeth as she and Kristen got into the car.

"And thanks again for the polish!" Kristen shouted out the window.

As I watched the car get farther and farther away, I felt as if the faint light of my personality was starting to shine through a little brighter.

CHAPTER 8

The first thing I saw when I walked into the salon on Saturday was Giancarlo in all his Giancarlo glory: a draped black and yellow gown ensemble that looked like a choir robe with slits up the sides, yellow pants underneath, and black leather slip-ons with a silver buckle.

"Wow, GC," I said. "That's really . . . something you have on there."

After stashing my bag and putting on my smock, I got my broom and started working. I was determined not to make a single mistake all day long and to stay completely focused on the task at hand. Then this happened:

"Has anyone seen a couple of bottles of the new spring polishes lying around anywhere?" Karen asked from her manicure station. "I'm out of two new colors and I've barely used them."

As you might imagine, this question kind of took me out of my zone.

"Not me," Giancarlo answered. "I only steal the cheese samples at Whole Foods."

"If they're free samples, then you're not stealing," Violet told him.

"Oh," Giancarlo said. "Rats. I thought I was being naughty."

"I did inventory myself just last weekend. I know they're back there. Maybe someone just moved them? Which colors are you looking for?" Violet said to Karen.

"Cornflower Blues and Peppermint Shake. Mickey, have you seen them?" Karen asked.

I could feel those evil little sweat monsters form over my upper lip. I shook my head no and casually said, "I think I saw some in the back on Wednesday." *Right before I swiped them.*

I wiped off some of the sweat, then looked for something to sweep up, trying to avoid eye contact with anyone.

"Well, they weren't there when I looked a minute ago."

"I'll definitely keep an eye out for them," I told Karen as I swept my way away from her.

The day calmed down a bit, even though the stream of clients stayed steady. Steady, except for Devon, that is. For the first part of the day I only saw her work on one client.

Giancarlo sat down his next client: a mom-age lady who was getting a trim and her gray roots touched up. "Mickey, darling," Giancarlo called to me. "Come grace us with your presence." I swept on over to him. "What do you think of Miss Lily here going for a brighter color, like blond?"

"Not blond!" Miss Lily said, clutching the ends of what I would call her dark, ash blond hair. "I don't want to look like Marilyn Monroe."

"Lily, honey, you wish," Giancarlo said. "I mean more of a honey blonde. Something a little spicier than the drab color you have now. If I look at it any longer I'm sure I'll slip into a coma."

"But I've been using this same color for fifteen years," she said.

He rolled his eyes. "Exactly. A lighter color will complement your skin tone much better. Right, Mickey?"

Giancarlo was probably just being nice by asking me, but I didn't care—I took the question seriously. When I looked at Miss Lily, something about her hair color (gray roots not included) and skin color did seem a bit off. I guess because it looked so unnatural together. Maybe a brighter color would work better.

"I think it'll look really pretty. Something punchier," I said.

"See?" Giancarlo said. "You can't say no to *punchier*. And you have to listen to her because she's Chloe's daughter."

Miss Lily eyed herself in the mirror and said, "Well, I guess it wouldn't hurt to try something new this once."

"Exactly!" Giancarlo said, clapping his hands together. "And your husband is going to love it!"

I went back to my sweeping, but not before Giancarlo gave me a thumbs-up. I didn't really think I'd done much to help, but it made me feel good anyway.

A little later, Jonah dropped by, skateboard in one hand and a paper bag in the other. "Your dad offered to give me some of those awesome homemade brownies if I agreed to take this to you. I think it's a tuna sandwich with an apple and a brownie," he said, handing me the bag, then coming behind the accessories counter like he owned the place.

"Thanks," I said, taking the bag while Jonah leaned on the glass counter. I swatted his forearm. "Get your sweaty arms off that. I was just about to clean it."

"Why does it matter what I get on it if you're about to clean it?"

"Because I don't want to come near your sweat

even through a rag and sterilized cleaning products."

"But you just touched me!"

"Just get out from behind here," I said, pushing his arm with my fingertips. "This space is for employees only."

"Well, excuse me," he said. "I didn't realize I was messing with . . . with . . ."

"With what?" I looked at Jonah. "Spit it out."

A girl about my age and her mom came into the salon and Megan greeted them right away. I didn't recognize her, and she looked like someone you'd remember if you saw her just once: She was super pale, super skinny, and had super light hair—almost white like Violet's, except this girl's was long and stick-straight.

"Hello, ladies!" Megan greeted them. As she checked the schedule, I noticed her side ponytail was tied with a band of clear wire with tiny red rosebuds. "You must be Mrs. Benton," Megan said to the mother, and to the daughter she said, "I'll bet you're Eve." Then Megan asked them if it was their first time at the salon and the mom explained that they'd just moved to town.

"Wow, great then," Megan cheered. "Violet and Giancarlo are just finishing up, so if you want to wait in the lounge, we'll get you when they're ready."

They sat down on the couch, each picking up a

magazine, and that's when I noticed Jonah was still looking at them, transfixed. When the girl looked up from her magazine, Jonah snapped around to me again, his eyes wide and his cheeks all flushed. "What's the matter with you?" I asked.

"Nothing," he said. "What's the matter with *you?*"

"Oh, brother," I said. I was not going to play this game with him, especially not while I was at work.

I wondered if Megan was going to ask Eve what school she was going to. I'd been totally embarrassed when she brought up school with Lizbeth and Kristen, but in this case I might not have minded it so much. Meanwhile, Jonah stood there like he was catatonic, Megan went back to her computer, and I didn't say another peep. So much for introductions.

I nudged Jonah's arm. "Seriously, are you okay?"

Just then Giancarlo made his way over to the reception area. "Who's my next pretty?" He turned to Jonah. "Is it your turn?" he asked. Then he scruffed up Jonah's hair and Jonah pulled his head away.

Eve dropped the magazine to the side and stood up. "I'm next," she said. She looked at Jonah. "Get in line, *pretty* boy," she said.

It was like, *whoa*, because we didn't even know who this girl was. And was she being serious or joking with Jonah? Kind of didn't matter, because she left him totally speechless.

"Goodness," Giancarlo said. "A girl with a little fire. I like it! Come on, sugar. I'll give you a style to match that personality."

Eve flashed us—or maybe just Jonah—a bright smile as she followed Giancarlo to his chair.

Jonah just stood there frozen for a moment before he said good-bye to me and left.

I watched as he walked out the door, dropped his skateboard to the sidewalk, and headed up Camden Way. Then he turned and skated back down on the slight slope toward home. He looked in our window as he passed, and I wondered what about that Eve girl had gotten him so tongue-tied.

CHAPTER 9

"What was your deal this afternoon?" I asked Jonah after dinner that night. We were sitting in his living room playing Warpath.

"What deal? I didn't have any deal," Jonah said.

"You just got very quiet when that girl Eve showed up. And you were kind of staring." Jonah blew up my entire fleet of choppers. "No big deal. So forget it."

"Fine, whatever."

Jonah finished off my last sniper and won the game. We tossed the controllers to the carpet.

"You know the new version of Warpath of Doom comes out this Thursday, right?" he asked. "Dad's taking me to get it after school. Do you wanna come with us and then come back home with me so we can play?"

"Sure, but be prepared for me to kick some booty," I told him. Then we played two more games before turning it off to watch an episode of *World's Dumbest*.

⋈ ⋈ ⋈

The next afternoon, most of the chairs were filled with women in various states of re-glamorization. The sounds of salon talk, hair dryers humming, and water running filled the air. Mom, who only took select clients since she had to run the whole place, was working on the mayor, who came in every six weeks for a trim and coloring. Word around the salon was that Mayor Gorman lost her first election because of her dated helmet hair and hint of a mustache. Everything changed, though, when she came into Hello, Gorgeous! She killed the next election.

I swept, cleaned, and fetched for the stylists and generally tried to stay out of trouble. I also did my best to avoid two people at the salon: Devon, who continued to ask me if I wanted her to cut my poor hair, and now Karen, who was still irked that her polishes had gone missing. I was beginning to regret ever taking those stupid bottles.

That morning had been pretty uneventful, but at about two o'clock in the afternoon, I heard two women squealing like a couple of sixth-graders who just found out they made the cheerleading squad. One was Giancarlo's client and one was Violet's.

"I haven't seen you since we filmed that cooking segment for the morning show!" Giancarlo's client said as she pulled in Violet's client for a hug.

"That must have been at least six months ago!" said Violet's client, hugging back. They each took their seats.

Piper had just finished up a cut, and, as she took her client to the front to pay, I swooped in to sweep her station, which was behind Giancarlo's. Today I would be a stealth sweeper, zapping away the mess before anyone could even spot me.

"I'll be back in two secs, Allyson," Violet said to her client.

"How's that girl of yours?" Beverly asked Allyson as Giancarlo began trimming the back of her hair.

"Oh, please," Allyson said, "she's a mess."

"Isn't every thirteen-year-old?" said Beverly.

My head popped up like a gopher from its hole when I heard them mention someone my age. I scooped up the pile of hair I'd been working on and quickly dumped it in Piper's wastebasket. I was supposed to take it to the trash in the back, but obviously I had more important things to do. Some people might have called it eavesdropping; I preferred *creative listening*.

I swept the floor so clean, you could have eaten pasta off of it. Neither of the women had a clue that I was paying any attention to them at all.

"You know girls. They want everything," Allyson said.

"You can't give in," Beverly said.

I pushed my broom across the center of the salon near Giancarlo's station. I knew I wasn't supposed to be sweeping while a client was in the chair, so I tried to stay outside the imaginary border of his station while staying within listening range.

Giancarlo shot me a sideways look, which I tried to ignore. "You're an eager little girl today," he said, finally.

The women stopped talking long enough to stare at me like I was trying to steal their purses.

"I thought I saw a, um, gum wrapper," I said.

"Mmmhmm," was all Giancarlo said. Then he went back to trimming Beverly's hair and she went back to talking. I stepped around to the other side of Violet's station, still within listening range.

"It just seems like a huge waste of money," Allyson said, getting up from her chair and inspecting her eyebrows in the mirror. "And not even practical. What's she even going to do with it?"

"Kids." Beverly said the word like it was a lemon on her tongue.

I leaned in toward Allyson, directing my broom strokes behind me, somewhere in the direction of mom's station. Suddenly, a metal crash sounded. I jumped, then realized I had knocked down several bottles from Mom's shelf, sending them clattering to the floor. The entire salon turned to stare at me.

My mother headed my way, looking like she was about to blow a fuse. "Just what are you doing?" she asked from between clenched teeth. If you've ever had a parent do that low, controlled angry voice, you know how terrifying it is. "Have I not yet explained that you're to refrain from sweeping around the stations while we're working on a client?"

I knew better than to answer her. Never make the mistake of answering a rhetorical question asked by an angry mother. She'll think you're being a smart aleck and ground you for sure. I say this from personal experience.

"I'm sorry," I muttered as I placed the products I'd knocked over back on her counter.

This was at least the third time I'd royally messed up at work, not including the petty theft incident. My stomach did a drop, and I wondered if I'd finally come to the end of my trial period at the salon.

"I mean, *I* didn't have a cell phone when I was in school, and I think I turned out just fine," Allyson was saying. "Besides, if Cara's head wasn't attached to her neck she'd lose that, too. I guarantee she'd lose that phone in a week."

Cara! Yes! A name!

"What does she need a phone for, anyway?"

Beverly said, as if it were a ridiculous thought, a kid wanting her own phone.

There was only one Cara in my grade—Cara Fredericks. She and her friends were really into drama and chorus. Honestly, it was kind of dumb logic for Allyson—now known as Mrs. Fredericks—not to get her daughter a cell phone just because she got along fine without one as a kid. Times have changed!

"What about you?" Mrs. Fredericks said. It took me a moment to realize she was speaking to me. "You look about my daughter's age."

"Allyson, have you not met Chloe's daughter?" Giancarlo asked. Violet had come back and began mixing color for Mrs. Frederick's hair. "This is Mickey. Ask her anything about hair, she'll give you a straight answer."

"Hello, Mickey," she said. "Nice to meet you. Do you know my daughter, Cara Fredericks?"

"Um, hi. Yes, I know Cara." I wasn't entirely sure she knew me, but that wasn't the question now, was it?

"Let me ask you: Do you have a cell phone?"

"Yes," I said. I had a phone, but I rarely used it. Mom and Dad were the only people I'd ever called or texted which, I realized right then, was kind of sad.

"Lots of kids have them," I added, trying to calm my shaking voice as Mrs. Fredericks, Beverly, and

Giancarlo all listened carefully. "I guess because, um, you know, maybe if we have to stay late at school for a project, or if we need to call our parents if something happens walking home from school or, like . . ." I kept going, remembering in my rambles that Cara had a little brother, "maybe if you needed Cara to pick up her brother at daycare. Or something."

"You know, you *can* find some pretty inexpensive phones," Beverly said. "For her first one, since she tends to lose things."

"Huh . . . I guess maybe I should think about it . . . ," Mrs. Fredericks said.

They didn't say anything more, but Giancarlo winked at me in the mirror as he went back to cutting Beverly's hair.

Wow, I thought. *Mrs. Fredericks is actually considering it. I* had helped change her mind. It felt pretty amazing, I had to admit. I vowed to try sharing my opinion more often.

That night after I showered, I sat at my vanity and brushed out my wet hair. Mom came into my room and all my excitement over convincing Mrs. Fredericks to reconsider the cell phone issue vanished. "Hi, honey," she said, sitting on my bed next to my vanity. "Can I talk to you about the salon?"

When she said *salon* I was sure she was talking

about the nail polishes. Her tone of voice was trying to lull me into a false sense of security, I just knew it. I wanted to pull out some excuse, like I had to go to bed immediately because of a new school policy that required every student to get ten hours of sleep. "Yeah, sure."

"First, I want you to know that I'm so happy you're taking an interest in what I do. It makes me very proud . . ."

That was nice and all, but I could hear a big *but* coming.

"*But* . . . (What'd I tell ya?) You've had a few slipups, haven't you?"

I felt like the turkey burgers and salt-and-vinegar chips from dinner were about to make a comeback all over my floor. I swallowed hard when I said, "I guess. I'm trying, though."

"I know you are. That means everything. And I know you love the salon—that's why I agreed to let you work there. But all the spills and mishaps have been disappointing. I can't have unnecessary distractions at my business. Do you understand?"

In case you haven't picked up on it yourselves, allow me to translate for you: *Mickey. You're doing a terrible job. Any other slipups, spilling, or spewing of sodas and you're toast.* Still, I was thankful she hadn't said anything about the polishes—yet.

86

"Yes," I told Mom. "I understand. I'm sorry. I really am trying."

"I know you are," she said. "Just pay a little more attention, okay?"

I hated that Mom had to call me out a second time, and so soon after the first. But I knew that if I were to survive, I'd have to shake it off. It wasn't too late to redeem myself, but the worst thing to do would be to let my confidence flag.

"Oh," Mom said before she left my room. "Karen said something about a couple of polishes that have gone missing. A light blue and a mint-green with pink sparkles? They're from the spring collection. Let me know if you see them around the salon."

"Okay," I said, my stomach clenching. So much for shaking anything off. I wondered how long until I was busted. Could someone please explain to me what I'd been thinking?

Well, thinking of nail polishes, when Mom left I pulled out a new slate-gray polish from my own stash. I painted my nails, but I was feeling so awful about her talk and the missing (stolen) nail polish that even though my nails were still wet, I suddenly wanted to go to bed. I put away the polish and turned off the lights. Then I carefully lay on my back and placed my nails outside the blanket, where they could dry while I slept.

CHAPTER 10

I woke up late the next morning to two surprises. Number one: I must have moved around in my sleep because my nails were covered in tiny little dents and marks from brushing against my blanket . . .

And number two: my hair, which also hadn't dried before I went to bed, was mushed up in a bird's nest in the back. I spritzed some water on it to try to get it to lay down properly, but then Dad yelled from downstairs to hurry up for breakfast. I grabbed a bottle of clear polish, thinking I could use it to smooth out the marks. When I left for school my hair was still a little wet and crazy and my nails were totally jacked. This didn't bode well for the rest of the day.

In homeroom I started putting on the clear polish, but Ms. Carter sniffed it out and made me put it away after I'd only gotten to one hand. At least my thumbnail looked slightly better.

At lunch, Jonah and Kyle were experimenting with making soda come out of their noses. I left early, thinking things couldn't get any worse.

Just before the bell rang in Ms. Carlisle's English class, a pale, ghostly girl walked through our doors and handed Ms. Carlisle a slip of paper. It was Eve, the girl from the salon! So she *was* going to Rockford after all! Ms. Carlisle pointed to a seat a row over from me, and as Eve crossed the room her wispy white hair fluttered behind her like a sheer curtain in the breeze. Giancarlo had left the length and had given her some long layers, and it had that healthy, just-cut bounce and shine to it.

Eve totally busted me staring at her as she sat down. "Hey! I know you," she said.

"Your hair looks really good," I responded. I couldn't believe how great it looked two days after the cut. And it wasn't the least bit oily, which meant she had to have washed it. Which meant that she had to have styled it by herself. I know life's not fair, but why was her hair so easy to style while mine was so impossible?

Eve sat down, putting her perfectly white backpack on the floor by her desk. "Thanks. I wanted to make a good first impression and everything."

"Cool," I said, trying to think of something else to say. *Mind . . . blank*.

"I'm Eve, by the way," she said, and I thought, *Right. That's one way to start a convo.*

"Oh, yeah, I actually overheard Megan, the receptionist, calling you Eve. I'm Mickey," I started. And then, I had a brilliant idea. "So you just moved here?"

Like, duh.

"How'd you know?" She smiled, showing me she was joking. "Yeah, from Connecticut. My mom wanted to be closer to her mom—she just had a stroke—so, here we are."

I told her I was sorry to hear it, and I started to work on the writing prompt Ms. Carlisle had just written on the board. She was having us write a story that used *pet mouse* and *hockey stick* in it. She does this sometimes because she says it's supposed to make us creative or something, but I think she uses it as an excuse to catch up on grading.

"Do you work at Hello, Gorgeous!?" Eve asked as if making conversation was so easy. Maybe it was, and I just spent too much time overthinking it.

"Yeah," I said. "It's my mom's salon."

"Awesome," she said. "You get free cuts and products and stuff?"

Great, I thought. This is the part where she asks me for a free flat iron and three-color process.

"I get some stuff," I said. "My mom cuts my hair,

but she won't do anything cool with it." I held up the ends of my hair to demonstrate the boringness of it.

We worked on our prompts some more. A little while later, Eve asked, "That guy you were talking to at the salon . . . the one with the skateboard?"

"Yeah," I said.

"Is he your brother?"

"My *brother*? No way. No, he's—"

And then I had a horrible thought that made me forget the pet mouse competing at the Olympic hockey match. "You don't think we look alike, do you?"

"No!" she said. "Not at all."

"Thank goodness," I said under my breath.

"Do you like him?" she asked.

What a weird question! "Of course," I told her. It'd be crazy if I didn't—I spent almost all my free time with him.

"Oh," was all she said, and then she turned back to her paper.

As I wrote about how hard it was for a mouse to push a hockey puck across the ice, it dawned on me. Eve was trying to figure out if Jonah was available. She wanted to know if I *liked* him-liked him before she made a move. I'd missed the whole meaning of it.

⋈ ⋈ ⋈

Later that day as I was heading to my last class, I

saw Lizbeth and Kristen walking together. I decided to be brave and speak up. I was allowed to do that, wasn't I?

"Hi, guys," I said.

"Hey," Lizbeth said when she saw me. I tried to think of more to say but . . . darkness . . . blankness . . . nothingness.

"Hey, have you heard about any pop quizzes lately?" Kristen asked me.

"No, not lately," I said. Then I managed, "I'll let you know if I do."

"Oh my gosh, your nails!" Lizbeth said, looking at the hand that clutched my books to my chest. They looked ridic.

"So cool!" she said. "How'd you do that?"

"Let me see," Kristen said, moving closer to my hand. "Oh, yeah. Texture. Really cool. And I love the color."

"*Love,*" Lizbeth said.

"Oh, this?" I said, looking at my nails. "It was kind of an accident. I went to sleep before they fully dried and I guess they got imprints from my pillow. If you see any gray in my hair, it's not from old age."

They laughed. "Well, it looks really cool," Lizbeth said.

"Thanks." I felt great. I was having a convo and making them laugh!

"We better go," Kristen said. "See you later?"

This time, it was more than just a way of saying good-bye. Kristen said it like a question, like they wanted to see me later.

"Yeah," I said, acting all cool. "See you later."

CHAPTER 11

Tuesday night, in my never-ending attempt to have hair that didn't look like a worn-out Brillo pad, I decided to try the flat iron.

We have a closet full of used supplies from the salon—old clips and barrettes that haven't been cool since I was in diapers, hair dryers that barely work, and a variety of curlers and flat irons. I think Mom just can't bear throwing out anything salon-related.

I took a medium-width one with a leopard-print handle and plugged it in at my vanity. Once it warmed up, I started smoothing out sections of my hair, one at a time.

"I smell death. With a side of vomit."

I looked in my mirror and saw Jonah looking back at me—half my hair sort of straight, the other half its usual frizz-ball self. "What's happening to your head?"

"I'm straightening my hair. What are you doing here?"

"I had nothing to do so I figured I'd come over here to bother you."

He does this a lot.

"Why are you changing your hair, anyway?" he asked. "It looks fine the way it is."

Obviously I like Jonah, but sometimes he just doesn't get it. Not that he tried to or anything. He just kept on talking without even pausing to give me a chance to answer him. Something about a new video game he saw on TV and how he was totally going to get it.

"And the game is, like, skateboarding meets bullfighting," Jonah rambled.

Taking hold of a section of hair at the back of my head, I pictured Eve's face as she asked me if I liked Jonah.

"It sounds like it might be even better than the new Warpath we're getting on Thursday, so we'll have to test them all out to see."

I thought I might try to casually bring Eve up to Jonah—test the waters a bit and see if he had any thoughts on her.

Keeping my eyes on myself in the mirror and sounding as cool as ever, I said, "There's this new girl in English class. I'm trying to get my hair to look like hers."

"And did I tell you I got a bullwhip? It is so awesome. You swing it around like this, and then it's like—*wha-bam*! So cool. I tried it in the house last night and almost broke half of everything in the living room. It was so awe—"

"She has really nice straight, smooth hair," I interrupted. He obviously didn't care about what I was saying, so I figured it was safe to keep talking over him. "Eve Benton—that's her name."

"*Wha-pah! Wha-bam!*" he yelled, still swinging his imaginary whip.

He just wasn't listening. "You know," I said forcefully, "that girl who was in the salon on Saturday? Super blond hair, almost white?"

He suddenly dropped his bullwhipping arm and took on an extremely casual manner, inspecting his palm like it held the secrets to the perfect whip-snap. "Oh, her. Yeah, I think I remember seeing her."

"Well then you must know how pin-straight her hair is."

"Haven't noticed," he said. "I'm a guy—remember?"

Sometimes he made it too easy. "No, I guess I didn't." Looking at myself in the mirror, I decided my hair was so difficult that I'd have to go over it twice to really smooth it out. I glanced at Jonah and could tell he was thinking about something other than bullwhips. "Actually, it's weird. She thought we were brother and sister."

"She mentioned my name?"

"How would she know your name? She just moved here. Besides, aren't you the least bit disturbed by that?"

"Well, what'd she say?" he asked.

"She asked if the guy with the skateboard was my brother."

"What else did she say?"

Jonah was trying so hard to seem casual, but he was failing at it so miserably.

"She asked me if I liked you."

"If *you* liked *me*? Well, what'd you say?"

"I told her I was madly in love with you and our parents had already decided we would marry next spring. What do you think I told her?"

"I was just asking."

"Why do you care so much, anyway? You don't even know what her hair looks like."

"I do so—it's long and so blond it's white and it's *straight*. Unlike some people's."

Okay. Total low blow.

I set down the flat iron and turned to look Jonah straight in the eye. "Do you like her?"

"I don't even know her!" Jonah said.

Which would have been believable had he not

contradicted himself immediately by saying: "Except she seems fun, like the way she trash-talked with me. Most girls are all stupid and giggly and stuff. *Oh, hee hee hee! My hair looks less than perfect.* But Eve is cooler than that!"

It was true, she *had* acted kind of, I don't know, brave at the salon, knocking Jonah around when she didn't even know him. I could never be that way with a person I'd just met.

"Well, tell me if you want me to say anything to her," I said.

"If you say *anything* to her, you're dead," Jonah said.

Boy, he must have it for her real bad.

CHAPTER 12

"Well, look at you."

I quickly tried to analyze the tone of Mom's voice the next morning, the flat look on her face. She liked it? She hated it? She thought I looked ultra-edgy but not in a good way?

"I used the flat iron," I said, sitting down at the table for breakfast. Mom's hair was mocking me more than ever, laying straight like a board down her back and tucked neatly behind her ears.

"Where'd you get the iron?" she asked, sipping her coffee.

"Found it in the closet."

"Honey, most of those should be thrown out. I'm not even sure why I keep them here."

Dad came into the kitchen to say good morning. He kissed my head, then paused and said, "Using new products or something?"

Did he wrinkle his nose when he said that?

"No product. I just straightened my hair," I said, refusing to doubt the two hours of work I'd put into it last night.

When Jonah popped over to walk with me to school, he didn't say anything about my hair—not that I expected him to—but he did manage to ramble on the entire way about entering a new level of Warpath of Doom.

"You're coming with me to the store tomorrow night, right?" he asked. "I'm creeping up on your score, so you better watch out!"

At school I tried to gauge the overall opinion on my hair. Was Stacey in history admiring it? What did Rebecca in science class mean when she said, "Oh. You straightened your hair." Ryan Majors walked past me and said, "What's that smell?"

Eve was the only person to flat-out say something nice to me. At least, I think she was being nice. When she saw me in class she said, "Cool. I like it when people try new things with their hair." Okay, it wasn't the same as saying she liked it, but she was complimenting me on something, at least.

I was walking down the hall after English class when I saw Lizbeth up ahead, kneeling on the ground. It looked like she'd dropped her bag, its contents splattered on the floor. I was about to bend down to help her when someone, some *guy*, went sailing practically over her leg.

When Lizbeth realized the guy was Matthew Anderson, her face turned pink and she looked stunned, paralyzed. She just sat there staring at him with wide eyes and a pack of spearmint gum in her hand. Tobias Woods, baseball stud and Matthew's best friend, stood by looking at his friend on the floor. He burst out laughing.

"Dude!" was all Tobias said.

If anyone knew how horribly embarrassed Lizbeth must have felt, it was me. The only difference between us was that I'd never made such a klutz of myself in front of my crush. That made it ten times worse. I had to help the girl out.

"Oh my gosh, I am such a mess!" I said to Matthew as he stood up, dusting off his perfectly pressed khakis. "I'm so sorry. Are you okay?"

Matthew looked at me and then back to Lizbeth, like he wasn't sure what was going on. "Yeah, I'm fine." He looked down at Lizbeth, still paralyzed on the floor.

"Did I get you, too?" I asked Lizbeth. She started to open her mouth, but nothing came out. "I am *such* a spaz. Two people at once—come on, guys, that's real talent! Let me help you." I bent down to help her. "Go with it," I whispered as I picked up the rest of the stuff from her bag—several pencils and tubes of lip gloss, a black, cloth headband, mint Tic Tacs, and scraps of paper.

"Hey, you okay, Lizbeth?" Matthew asked. She looked up at him and nodded. Apparently she'd lost her voice. "'Kay. Well, see you."

Tobias clapped Matthew on the back and laughed some more as they walked away.

After he'd left, Lizbeth let out a deep breath and said, "Oh my gosh, that was totally embarrassing! It was bad enough I let my bag spill out all over the freaking school, but then I totally tripped Matthew! I am dying!"

She paused for a second and then gave me a quizzical look. "Why'd you cover for me like that?"

I shrugged, thinking of my spectacular fall at the salon. "I have lots of experience with falling, unfortunately. I know how it feels. Except, I guess I've never sent someone else to the ground. You were like a human bowling ball taking down his pin."

Lizbeth laughed, putting her hand over her face. "Awful. But thanks. I owe you."

We finished putting her things back in her bag and then we stood up. "No, you don't. Sometimes you just gotta take one for the team."

"Thanks, Mickey," Lizbeth said as she pulled me in for a quick hug.

At the end of last period I spotted a huddle of girls with their heads together. When I got closer I saw that they were crowded around Cara Fredericks, who was showing them something—something that glowed a light blue in her face. It was—

A cell phone!

"You got it!" I said without thinking as they gathered around to take a picture. Really, I couldn't believe it. Cara's mom actually got her a phone. Could it have been because of what I had said to her?

Cara and her friends turned to look at me, no doubt wondering what I was talking about.

"Oh, um," I began. "I saw your mom in the salon. Where I work. At Hello, Gorgeous! She was asking about cell phones and stuff."

"Mickey, hey," Cara said. "My mom said she talked to someone from school. That was you?"

"Yeah," I answered. I tried to act cool and casual when I said, "We talked about it—phones and stuff." Like a superhero, it was Mickey to the rescue!

"Thank you so much!" Cara said. "I seriously thought I would be the last person on earth to get a cell phone."

"Don't forget me, Cara," her friend Maggie Williams said. She had sunset-red hair, a perky nose, and long lashes. "I still don't have one. Hey, Mickey, do you think you could talk to my mom, too?"

"Um, well . . ." What had happened with Cara's mother could have been a fluke. There was no guarantee it would work on someone else. "Is your mom coming in or something?"

"Well, no," Maggie said. "But maybe I can tell her to get an appointment. What do you say? Your mom would get a whole new customer out of it."

I could have said no to Maggie since I barely knew her, but if I did her this favor it'd be a way to get to know her, right? Plus, I was pretty much on a roll, first with helping out Lizbeth and then with Cara. Now both of them seemed more interested in me. "What does your mom look like?" I asked Maggie. "I'll put in a good word for you."

She held the ends of her hair. "She's a redhead, like me. People say I'm a mini version of her." Maggie rolled her eyes, like she was pretending not to like it but maybe sort of did. "Oh my gosh, thank you so much!"

"Sure," I said. Then I turned to Cara. "Want me to take a picture for you?" I asked her.

"Totally," she said, handing over her shiny, new phone to me.

I pointed the camera at them and got ready to click. "Now everybody say *gorgeous*!"

It was hair as usual at the salon that afternoon, but I couldn't get the polishes off my mind. The good news, though, was that no one seemed to be thinking about it but me.

"Oh, for heaven's sake, what *is* that smell?" Giancarlo asked as I walked past his station. He'd been drying a woman's hair, her blondness blowing around her face. All she needed was a mic and a stage and she'd have been pop-star ready.

For a moment, I thought Giancarlo was talking about me and that weird flat iron smell. But no. It would have been impossible for him to smell with me just drifting by. No way.

"Mickey, darling, is that *you*?" he asked, his nose wrinkled.

"No!" I said. Loudly. And defensively. "I mean, ha-ha, no, nope, nu-uh, not me. Why would you think that? I mean, what smell? I mean, what?"

Spiraling, spiraling, spiraling . . .

"That acrid, chemical smell that has completely offended my senses," he said, turning off the dryer and taking a step toward me in white, patent boat shoes. Looking more closely at my hair he said, "It smells like burnt hair. Did you burn your hair? Wait, what *did* you do to your hair?"

And suddenly I wanted to cry from embarrassment.

The straightening had been a total bust and it was obvious to everyone. But I was still too embarrassed to admit it.

"I didn't do anything," I said.

"Yes, you did."

It was Devon, listening from all the way across the salon. She was the only one not working, sitting in her chair like she owned the place. Actually, not even Mom would ever sit in her own chair. And she certainly didn't allow her stylists to laze around like that. So where was she now to tell Devon to chop-chop?

"You flat ironed it," Devon oh-so-helpfully informed me. "And it smells like burnt hair and your hair looks like, well, like you tried an iron on it, an iron that's either old or not very good in the first place. Or maybe you used it on too high a setting. What setting did you use?"

"None," I said, heading to the back to get changed and get to work and away from all the prying eyes.

"You know, Mickey," Devon called as I left the floor. "I know you don't believe me, but I could solve all your hair problems with just one sitting in my chair. I've got my scissors all sharpened and ready!"

Yeah. She wished. Anyway, I wasn't letting her *or* my hair get me down. By the time I snapped on my smock and got back out on the floor (after pulling my hair back in a messy bun and spritzing it with a nice raspberry hairspray), I was ready to work. No mistakes, no mess-ups, nothing. I'd had too many already and it was time to be totally perfect.

And you know what? I pretty much was. I swept but didn't get in the stylists' way. I kept the accessories counter and drinks area neat, clean, and shiny. At around seven thirty, Megan felt like it was time to do a drawing and had me draw a name from the fishbowl. She cheered when I read the name—Julie Acton—even though the winner wasn't there and no one knew who she was. I even gave some advice to one of our oldest clients (in age and in loyalty) about adding a pink streak to her hair. Violet said it was a little extreme; I said she'd look awesome. She went with it and left the salon happier than she'd been after any other visit.

I just might go so far as to say the day was one of my best yet. Aside from my hair debacle, I was on a roll.

CHAPTER 13

The next day I admitted defeat (but only to myself) by doing nothing more than washing and drying my hair. As Jonah and I walked down the tree-lined sidewalks of our neighborhood and turned left onto the long narrow road to school like we did almost every morning, I felt better than I had in a while. The night before, as Mom and I left the salon together, she'd bumped my hip and said, "Nice job tonight." I'd grinned a big, crazy grin and felt so proud that she had noticed.

"Tonight's the night," Jonah said as we approached school. "We're going to pick up the new game and christen it, so don't forget."

"Mickey! Hey! How's it going?" Maggie Williams waved from across the school lawn, her flaming red hair fluttering around her face.

"Who's that?" Jonah asked.

"Maggie," I said as I waved back and said hello. Feeling bold, I told Jonah, "My friend."

"Yeah, right," he muttered. I was pretty sure he was just joking, but I didn't exactly love the tone. Like I couldn't have friends of my own?

Like I *could*. I *totally* could.

At lunch, Jonah and Kyle dived face-first into the spaghetti special, hands behind their backs. They gobbled up what passed for marinara and meatballs while I watched in horror. Their faces were quickly covered in sauce and bits of faux meat. I would have turned away, but I had been charged with the distinct honor of calling the winner. If I had any chance of breaking out and making new friends, I was pretty sure they'd just been demolished.

People around us were staring. It was humiliation overload. I looked across the cafeteria where Lizbeth and Kristen sat, and I saw Lizbeth look our way, but she didn't seem to see me. That was one thing to be thankful for.

"Done! Done!" yelled Jonah, a stranded string of spaghetti dangling off his chin.

"Nice, dude," Kyle said, slapping hands with Jonah. I had to admit, I didn't know Kyle had it in him to do something that could land him in detention. Eating like a pig out of a trough wasn't exactly the coolest move but, for some reason, I was impressed.

And totally grossed out.

"Can I go vomit now?" I asked.

"Not till you declare me the winner," Jonah said. He held out his hand as if he expected me to raise it in victory.

"I'm getting some ice cream," I said, standing. I needed an excuse to get away from those two, and ice cream seemed like the perfect one.

I took a sandwich out of the bin and stood in line.

"That was kind of insane," a voice behind me said. When I turned and saw that it was Lizbeth, I wanted to crawl into the ice cream barrel and hide until final bell. She *had* seen.

"Oh. Um, hi," I muttered, feeling my neck flush red, the color easing its way up to my face. I didn't want to be ashamed of my best friend, but I couldn't exactly brag about him, either, now could I? Not after that display.

"You gotta hand it to them," Lizbeth said. She picked an ice cream sandwich out of the bin. "Even just eating that food is probably, like, hazardous to their health."

I smiled. "They're probably foaming at the mouth right about now. I should go check on them," I said, then stood purposely still and gazed up at the water-stained ceiling like I had all the time in the world. Lizbeth laughed.

We inched our way toward the cashier to pay. "So," she said, tucking an escaped strand of hair from her messy bun. "Thanks again for saving me in the halls with Matthew. I was *so* mortified."

"No biggie," I said. "If you ever need me to take someone out on purpose, I can do that, too. I'm, like, full-service that way."

Lizbeth laughed again as we moved up in the line. "You going to the baseball game tonight?"

Baseball game? Tonight? "I'm not sure," I lied. Totally, one hundred percent lied because I hadn't been to a single sports game all year and, until two seconds ago, had no plans to go anytime soon. "It's a home game," she said. "Kristen and I are going. You should come."

It was kind of like an out-of-body experience. I saw myself nodding my head and saying, "Yeah, maybe I will."

"Cool. You're up." She nodded ahead of me to the register.

Once I paid for my ice cream I realized I had to go call my dad and tell him I'd be home late from school, and my phone doesn't get reception in the cafeteria. Since we're not allowed to eat outside the cafeteria, I brought the sandwich over to Jonah and dropped it on the table in front of him. "Your prize for winning," I said.

"Thanks! Hey, where're you going?" he asked as I kept walking toward the door.

"I gotta make a phone call!"

After clearing it with Dad, I bounded through my final classes of the day, excited and nervous about my sudden after-school plans.

When Eve walked into English class, she smiled at me and said hello. The aqua-blue pleated skirt and pink polo she wore made her look like she was ready for the tennis courts. I went into my usual mini freak-out over what to say to her. I thought of Jonah the other day and his weirdness about her and how I could do a little more digging to see if they liked each other. Then I thought of Jonah doing a spaghetti face-plant and wondered if it was for the best to just leave it alone, at least for now.

I was completely capable of making non-Jonah-related conversation. I totally could do it. All I had to do was *say* something. Something simple. Anything.

"Hi."

Sadly, that was the best I could come up with.

"What's up?" Eve said, dropping her bag on the floor by her desk. Everyone made it seem so easy to talk to people they didn't know—so why was I sweaty and palpitating?

"Are you going to the baseball game after school?"

Following her question with a second question was another option.

Eve pulled a light blue folder out of her bag. "I didn't know there was a game," she said because why would she know? She'd been here exactly four days.

I tried to act as casual as Lizbeth had when she asked me. "Oh, yeah. Baseball. They're playing here tonight. You should come."

"Well, I have to go to my grandma's after school, so—maybe next time? Do you know when the next game is?"

Of course not, since I've never had any interest in it at all until twenty-seven minutes ago. "I'm not sure," I said. "But I can check."

"Cool," she said, pulling papers out of her notebook as Ms. Carlisle passed out a worksheet for us.

That went well. We chatted. We made tentative plans. Working at the salon was having a positive effect on my personality.

In that it was giving me one.

After school I slipped into the ladies' room, redid my ponytail, and added a skinny headband with a Spanish red flower on the side. It was a warm sunny day and slightly breezy, and I wanted to keep my hair out of my face. Except really, I wanted to look good.

As I walked out to the bleachers I had a fluttering of nerves in my stomach. What if they didn't invite me to sit with them? What if they totally ignored me and I had to sit by myself? What if, worse, they thought I was clinging and pathetic and stalking them?

Dad once said something that now rang in my ears: Fake it till you make it. Like, pretend what's bothering you really doesn't bother you. Soon enough, it won't for real. So I walked across the field to the bleachers like it was something I did every day.

I saw them sitting together in the stands. Should I sit near them? Ask to sit by them? Ignore them in case I looked pathetic? Truly, my thoughts were exhausting.

Parents and students settled on the bleachers as the players warmed up on the field. I took one step up, spotted an empty place to sit, and headed for it.

"Hey, Mickey," Kristen called out. Her red-and-white-striped shirt fluttered in the warm breeze.

"Hi." I waved, relieved that one of them had said something.

"Cute headband," Lizbeth called.

"Thanks," I said, reaching up to touch the little flower that was slightly smashed from being in the bottom of my bag.

"Did you get it at your mom's salon?" Lizbeth asked.

"Yeah." I was standing on the bleachers, blocking some poor father's field of vision. "That's so cool,"

Kristen said. "You're so lucky you get to work there."

"Yeah," I said. "It's pretty cool." Bold. I felt a rush of bold. Kind of like when I decided to go for it and reference Matthew Anderson to Lizbeth. Observe:

"Can I sit with you guys?"

A pause that lasted for eternity hung in the air.

Lizbeth scooted over a bit on her seat. "Sure."

And just like that, I was sitting with them.

"Let's go, Ravenclaws!" Kristen cheered loudly. Lizbeth laughed and nudged her in the arm.

"You're such a dork," she told her. "They're just warming up."

"Well, they're doing a really good job of it. Especially Tobias Woods." Kristen cupped her hands around her mouth and yelled, "Looking good, Tobias!"

"Oh my gosh, you are so embarrassing!" Lizbeth laughed, and I did, too.

When the game started I clapped and cheered and *woohoo*-ed along with Lizbeth, Kristen, and the rest of the people in the stands.

The girls watched the game a little, but only to watch Tobias. He played shortstop, and in case it wasn't noticeable, Kristen had a crush on him.

"It's new," she told me. "It all started last weekend when I was at Scoops on Camden Way. I had just ordered the Dulce de Leche when someone"—she eyed Lizbeth—"knocked it from my hands."

"Please!" Lizbeth said. "You bumped into me."

(Lizbeth sure did a lot of tripping and bumping and dropping. From the sound of it, she was almost as big a klutz as me. Something to note for future bonding purposes.)

"Anyway," Kristen continued, "Tobias saw what happened and straight up bought me a new cone. Without even asking. I hadn't really noticed him much before then, but now . . ." She sighed. "I've noticed."

"Cool," I said. "Does he know you like him?"

"He does now," Lizbeth said.

We watched the game for a few minutes until Kristen had an important sighting. "Lizbeth, look," Kristen said. She was pointing back toward the school. We all looked to see Matthew Anderson crossing the field to the bleachers. Tonight he was wearing a Harvard sweatshirt with tan boat shoes.

"Please don't embarrass me," Lizbeth said to Kristen.

"Lizbeth," Kristen loudly whispered. "Think of the double dates!"

"I'd be so mad at you right now if she didn't already know," Lizbeth said, motioning to me.

Kristen looked around at me. "Lizzie told me. Nice save, taking the fall for Grace here."

I shrugged, blushed, grinned. "No biggie."

Matthew took a seat on the bleachers two rows down and a bit over from us. Mostly out of earshot, as long as no one spoke too loudly.

"Hi, Matthew!" Kristen called, and Lizbeth buried her face in her hands. Even though most of her face was covered, it was obvious she was embarrassed. "Come to cheer Tobias on?"

"Hey, Kristen," Matthew said. Looking at me and Lizbeth he said, "Hello, ladies."

"Oh my gosh," Lizbeth muttered, still hiding her face.

"Do you want to come sit with us?" Kristen asked. "Plenty of room here." She patted the tiny space between her and Lizbeth.

He smiled, flashing white teeth. "I'm not staying long. I have tennis lessons at the club in half an hour."

What'd I tell you? Total prep.

"Cool," Kristen said. "Well, we're here if you need us!"

"Thanks," he said.

Everyone went back to watching the game except Lizbeth. She whacked Kristen in the arm and said, "I can't believe you just did that!"

"Lizzie, why do you always act so weird around boys?"

"I only act weird when you purposely humiliate me," Lizbeth said.

"You embarrass yourself by acting embarrassed," Kristen said. "You need to chill out. Guys are *so* not that big of a deal. Ask Mickey. She's best friends with one of them."

"Eh. They're not that bad. If you don't mind the occasional burps in your face and incessant talk about skateboards and video games."

"See?" Kristen said. "The worst that can happen is he could blow burps in your face."

After just a little while Matthew got up to leave. He couldn't even get both feet on the ground before Kristen was calling, "Bye, Matthew! See you tomorrow! Lizbeth says good-bye, too!"

"Kristen!" she snapped, covering her face again. Kristen laughed, and I sort of did, too, but it was super clear that Lizbeth didn't think it was funny at all. I felt bad for her. Kristen did seem a little pushy.

Lizbeth reached into her bag, took out some lip gloss, and swiped it across her lips. Without a word she passed it to Kristen, who did the same. And poof, without one word exchanged, they were all made up.

Kristen held the lip gloss out to me. At that moment, looking at Kristen's hand holding the glittery tube for me, I felt like I was in. Maybe not Friday-nights-level-in, but in nonetheless.

I took the gloss—Sugar Cane Sheer with tiny little silver specks in it—and swiped it across my lips, grinning a glittery grin for the rest of the game.

The next morning I decided to forgo my usual ponytail and try wearing two long braids. Then, I was almost late to school because I waited for Jonah to show up so we could walk to school together like we did every morning. I called his house but no one answered, so I finally had to leave without him.

Maybe in a way it was for the best, because I ran into Lizbeth and Kristen jumping out of Lizbeth's mom's car. We all raced up the steps at the same time. Before they went one way and I went the other, Lizbeth called back, "Sit with us at lunch, if you want."

If I wanted? I stood completely still in the hall, stunned, staring into space. First the baseball game and now lunch—which was huge. Friday nights might not have been as far off as I thought they were.

I usually saw Jonah at some point during morning classes, but that day I didn't. I was beginning to think that he was sick, but then I saw him walking toward the cafeteria for lunch. He was with Kyle and they were probably going to have one of their usual gross-out fests. Thank goodness I would be spared from whatever they had in store today. I figured everyone would be happier with me sitting at another table and leaving them to their business. Me, especially.

I waited for Lizbeth and Kristen outside the cafeteria. When I saw Eve, I asked her if she wanted to eat lunch with us.

"Yes, please," she said, looking relieved. "I hid out in the library the first two days and then graduated to the cafeteria where I sat with some girls who worked on their sticker collections at lunch. Don't get me wrong—they were nice and all, but I haven't traded stickers since the second grade."

"Well," I said, feeling bold, "you're with us now."

"Have you guys met Eve yet?" I asked when Lizbeth and Kristen showed up. "She just moved here this week."

Then Lizbeth and Kristen introduced themselves and we headed toward their table. As we crossed the cafeteria, Jonah spotted me. I was glad he was at school and okay, but wondered why he had bailed on me that morning. He held up his hands to me like, *What are you doing?* and I held up my own like, *What do you want me to do?*, then followed the girls to their table.

"Do you three have any classes together?" Eve asked.

"No," Lizbeth said. "We met at her mom's salon."

"*We* met at her mom's salon, too!" Eve said, sitting down. "And, wait, can we talk about how cool it is that her mom owns that salon?"

"So cool," Lizbeth agreed. "She gets all the best hair products and accessories."

"And nail polishes," Kristen added.

I smiled—beamed, really. Yeah, it was pretty cool. The salon, the compliments, the hanging out.

It was all going pretty darn well.

CHAPTER 14

When I got to the salon on Saturday, I stuck my head in my mom's office to let her know I was there. When I opened the door, I saw Devon sitting across from her desk. They both turned to look at me.

"Oh, sorry," I said, stepping back out again. Mom had her hands folded on her desk, and Devon sat tightly, her knees glued together and her arms wrapped around her ribs. I wondered if she was sick. "Just wanted to let you know I'm here."

"Thanks, Mickey. I'll be out in a minute."

"Okay," I said, stepping back out. I almost shut the door completely, but then . . . well, then I wondered what was going on. I had noticed that lately Devon hardly had any clients, and I wondered if their talk had anything to do with that. She'd had some at first, but they'd dwindled down to almost nothing. Even new clients didn't seem to want her to work on them.

". . . you're new, but we really need to address the problem," Mom was saying. Devon mumbled something that sounded like "I know," but it was hard to hear. She was usually so outspoken, but now her voice seemed to be stifled. Mom continued, "I don't want to have to give your station away, but if things don't improve . . ."

Wow. Getting your station taken away meant getting fired. I hadn't realized things were that bad. I felt sorry for Devon—I didn't want anyone to get in that much trouble.

I heard rustling in Mom's office and made a quick dash for the back. I ditched my stuff, snapped on my smock, and got out on the floor. I was rearranging some towels when Devon came out looking red in the eyes. She kept her head down as she walked back to her station, her studded wedges stomping with determination. Violet and Giancarlo seemed to make a point of not looking at her by turning away from her area completely. They had to have known what was happening.

I grabbed my broom and pretended to get to work. When I passed Piper's station, I quietly asked her what was going on.

"No clients, no money," Piper said out of the side of her mouth, like she didn't even want Devon to know she was talking.

I watched as Devon sprayed her mirror with glass cleaner and wiped it down, then ran the wet paper towel around the leather of the chocolate-brown frame. She'd had so few clients that her products could have easily been collecting dust, but one thing you could say for her was that her station was sparkling clean.

Our eyes caught, and I smiled more brightly at her than I ever had. Instead of yelling at me that I should let her cut my hair, she gave me a barely-there smile on her crimson-less lips. She looked sad and defeated.

When Mom came out of her office, we all went quickly back to work. Devon finished cleaning and stood stoically beside her station, almost daring anyone to sit in her chair. She didn't exactly look inviting, but maybe she figured it was better than looking desperate.

It was so beautiful outside that we had fewer customers than we did on other Saturdays. The day passed slowly with customers trickling in and out practically one at a time. Devon didn't have to feel so bad—even Giancarlo only had a couple of clients, and he usually stayed almost as busy as Violet.

In the late afternoon, Megan got bored and did some homework, which Mom said was fine as long as she kept it discreet. Mom was cutting a woman's espresso-colored hair, and they chatted about a new chef in town and whether or not the food was worth the hype.

I was up near the front when Lizbeth and her mom

walked through the doors. I had no idea they were coming.

"Hey there," I said, trying not to sound too eager and excited.

"Hi, Mickey," she said. I liked her outfit—pale pink Hello Kitty T-shirt, ripped jeans, and blue flip-flops.

Megan greeted them, pulling a hair magazine over her textbook before pulling up the scheduling program on the computer. "Here for a cut?"

"Just manicures," Lizbeth's mom said. Her hair was a brighter blond (courtesy, no doubt, of a little help from the girls at Hello, Gorgeous!) than Lizbeth's own honey blond. She wore a thin gold watch that she twisted around her freckled wrist, and she had a polite smile.

"We only have Karen on duty today. Is that okay?" Megan asked. When Mrs. Ballinger said it was fine, Megan instructed them to pick out their colors and have a seat at the manicure station. She got on the house phone and called Karen up from the break room while Mrs. Ballinger chose a sheer white. Lizbeth looked at the drawing fishbowl and picked up the pen we kept next to the entry forms.

"Is there an age limit for this?" she asked.

"Nope," I said. "Go for it."

"Cool." She filled out two cards and dropped them in a bowl. "One for Kristen," she said. Then added,

"By the way, I heard you got Cara a cell phone. That's pretty cool."

I shrugged, playing like it was no big deal, but inside—I felt pretty cool. Karen came up as Lizbeth and her mom sat down. Mrs. Ballinger gave Karen the sheer white, and, from her bag, Lizbeth pulled out a color from her purse—Peppermint Shake.

I almost dropped my broom.

"Hey, where'd you get that?" Karen asked.

"I got it from—," she said, turning to point to me. I shook my head frantically in tiny little jerks—the international sign for *ix-nay on the olish-pay.* How could I have forgotten to tell her and Kristen to keep their polish away from my mom? "From a store," Lizbeth said, keeping one eye on me. I did the head shake again. It wasn't even in stores yet. Lizbeth's eyes widened and she stammered, "I mean a gift. I got it as a gift. From a friend." She looked at Karen and plastered a smile on her face.

I could see Violet watching us from the corner of my eyes. Devon, who'd been hanging around with Violet at her station, was watching, too.

"Well, hold on to it," Karen said to Lizbeth. "Apparently it's a hotter ticket than even I thought," she said. Then she took a slightly closer look at her and asked, "Did I ever use it on you . . . ?"

Lizbeth wrapped her fingers tightly around the mint-green and pink bottle, sliding her eyes toward me.

"Uh, Karen!" I called. She turned to look at me as Lizbeth shot me a questioning look. I stepped closer to the station and said, "Um, just wondering if you needed anything. Do you need anything? Anything at all?" What I said didn't matter as long as I distracted her from the interrogation.

"No, Mickey," Karen said, grabbing a cotton ball and putting nail polish remover on it. "I'm good."

A moment later, Lizbeth put the mint-green nail polish back in her bag and told Karen that she had changed her mind about the color and wanted to go with a sheer pink instead. Brilliant move on the part of Lizbeth—hiding the evidence. Talk about taking it for the team.

I let out a breath as Karen began working on Mrs. Ballinger's nails. I couldn't tell if she was onto me. Mom was in deep discussion mode with her client and I didn't think she'd overheard any of our conversation, but I couldn't be sure. It was all so nerve-wracking.

"I'm heading to CJ's," Megan said once I'd saved myself from getting busted, fired, and humiliated on the spot. In front of my new friend. Who didn't look too thrilled with me at the moment. "Will you watch the front for me? Your mom will be right there if you need anything."

"Yeah, sure," I said, leaning my broom against the wall. I felt terrible, like some petty little lowlife thief, which I guess I was. That whole polish thing had been such a huge mistake, and now to top it off, I had made Lizbeth my unsuspecting accomplice. "Be back in two flat," Megan said, sending a breeze through the doorway as she walked out.

Mom finished up with her client and escorted her to reception. The woman, whose hair now framed her face in perfect wisps, paid and made an appointment for six weeks out, just as my mom suggested. When the woman left, I braced myself as I waited for her to say something about the polishes.

"Everything okay?" she asked.

"Yes," I said.

Mom smiled, then gazed out the window for a second. "I don't have anything else today. I think I'll get back in my office and do some number-crunching."

I let out a deep but quiet breath. The smile was a good sign. It meant she probably hadn't heard. As she passed me, she tucked some wiry strands behind my ear. "Violet's right here if you need anything."

Violet looked over at me again, but I couldn't tell if there was anything behind the look other than just, you know, *looking* at me. I smiled at her, anyway, just in case.

I leaned on the reception desk and played the nail

polish scene over and over in my head. There was a good chance Karen had figured out how Lizbeth got the polish. The question was whether or not she'd tell my mother. *Telling your boss that her daughter is a petty thief is probably not the quickest way to a pay raise,* I reasoned. *At least I ho—*

Suddenly my thoughts were interrupted by an intriguing conversation between Lizbeth and her mother. "We paid a lot of money for that table."

"Yeah, but why do I have to go to some boring fund-raiser at the country club? They play horrible music and everyone gives us dirty looks if we laugh too loud," Lizbeth said.

I shifted my body ever so slightly. I wasn't trying to eavesdrop; I was just trying to get more comfortable.

"Stop complaining," Lizbeth's mom said. "You'll get a new dress out of it, plus we can have a girls' afternoon and get our hair done beforehand. It'll be fun!"

Ah, yes. The old "just by saying it'll be fun will make it true" routine. I'd heard that one before. When I was in third grade, Dad tried to convince me that playing softball would be fun. I fell for it and ended up benched for most of the games because I complained about hat hair. I hoped Lizbeth wouldn't make the same mistake I did.

Lizbeth was silent. She must have been thinking

about it. "Who's going to be there?" she asked.

"The Andersons and their son Matthew, and the Woodses and their son Tobias. Those two families are the best of friends, and now your father and I have gotten to know them a bit ourselves."

Matthew Anderson? I thought.

"Matthew *Anderson*?" Lizbeth asked.

"Yes. Do you have classes with him?"

Lizbeth didn't answer, but I could hear the tiny hint of a smile in her voice. How lucky was she to be going to the same fund-raiser as her crush and sitting at the exact same table? "So now you're setting me up on dates, huh, Mom?"

Mrs. Ballinger practically gasped. "It most certainly is not a date. It's just three families sharing a table at a benefit. A very expensive table. And the boys just happen to be your age." After a moment, she said, "Matthew—is he cute?"

"Mom!"

"Okay, fine. You're the one who called it a date. Invite Kristen and you'll have a great time. Just remember that this is a very important dinner to your father," Lizbeth's mom continued. "You and Kristen need to be on your best behavior."

Lizbeth didn't say anything more and soon her mom was talking about the Andersons and their winter vacation in the Florida Keys.

Megan finally returned, her cheeks extra rosy. "Here," she said, dropping a bag on the counter. "Thanks for covering for me."

"Thanks," I said, looking inside the bag—two chocolate chip, peanut butter cookies.

I got my broom, which was leaning against the wall, and tried to think of something else to clean or straighten up. I was wiping down the shelves that held products for sale when Lizbeth called from the door, "Hey, Mickey! I'll talk to you Monday, okay?"

Did *talk* mean just that we'd see each other on Monday or did it mean that she wanted to *talk* talk about the polish? My stomach cramped up just thinking about it.

Lizbeth waved good-bye—or maybe she was just trying to dry her colored nails—and headed out the door.

If only I hadn't taken those nail polishes—how on earth could I have thought that was a good idea?

CHAPTER 15

As I got dressed for school on Monday, I mentally prepared myself to talk to Lizbeth about the polish sitch. I wanted to smooth the whole thing over so we could all have a nice, leisurely lunch talking about clothing and boys. At least talking to Lizbeth would be a lot easier than talking to my mother. It seemed like I was out of the woods from being a prime suspect in the case of the missing spring polishes, since Mom hadn't said anything to me last night.

Downstairs Dad served up fresh blueberry pancakes and scrambled eggs for breakfast. "The Goldmans just called. Jonah's mom is driving him to school today, so don't worry about waiting for him," he told me.

I poured maple syrup over the pancakes. "That's weird. I didn't see him all weekend and he totally bailed on me on Friday. I wonder if he's mad at me."

I speared the pancakes and took a bite. Blueberry deliciousness popped in my mouth.

"I'm sure he'll explain it to you when you see him," Dad said.

When the lunch bell rang I dashed to the cafeteria to meet up with Lizbeth, Kristen, and Eve. I waited outside the doors to the lunchroom, looking over the tops of heads and keeping an eye out for everyone. Jonah got there first.

"Oh, hey, Jonah," I said.

"Hi," he said. He shoved his hands in his baggy jeans pockets and scanned the cafeteria. It almost seemed like he was pretending to look for someone so he could avoid looking at me.

"Where've you been these last couple of mornings? Is your alarm clock broken or something?" I asked.

"No," he said with a giant edge to his tone. "My alarm clock isn't broken."

"Then where were you?" He shrugged his shoulders—he didn't know where he'd been? I wanted to ask him if he was mad at me, but I didn't want to cause a whole drama-fest outside the cafeteria. Plus, I had just caught sight of Kristen's auburn hair coming my way.

"Listen, Mickey, I gotta—"

"We should talk," I interrupted. Jonah didn't say

a word. "But don't worry about saving me a seat today, I'm gonna sit with my friends."

Okay, I have to admit I loved using that term—*my friends*. Especially the *s* part. As in more than just one.

"Hey, Mickey. What's up, Jones?" Kristen said to Jonah. He shot her a look, then headed into the caf.

"Jonah!" I called, but he ignored me.

"What's his deal?" Kristen asked, looking a little confused.

"I'm not really sure," I said. Maybe he didn't like that I was hanging out with the girls and not him? I couldn't imagine that he'd care, but maybe he did.

"I love your purse," I told Kristen, pushing thoughts of Jonah out of my mind. It was silver with a silver chain and a fat rose bloom on the front.

"Thanks," she said. "I just saw Eve—she said she's not coming to lunch because she has to see her history teacher." Kristen's eyes widened. "So . . . I heard about what happened this weekend . . ."

"Oh yeah . . . about the fund-raiser, you mean?"

"Huh?" she said.

"At the country club with Lizbeth's family. Lizbeth was in the salon on Saturday with her mom talking about it. Have you thought about what you're going to wear? I'll totally help you with your hair if you want."

"Mickey, *what* are you talking about?" she asked—very firmly, I might add.

"The fund-raiser at the country clu . . ." I let my voice trail off then. The look on Kristen's face said it all. It had seamlessly gone from one of curiosity into one of vengeful anger.

My stomach dropped and my heart raced. What had I just done? Why had I thought it was a good idea to, you know, *talk* to people? Kristen glared at me, her cheeks turning bright red. This was so not good.

"Um, actually, I think I was thinking of someone else," I backpedaled, desperately wanting to make this conversation go far, far away. "I heard someone else talking about . . . some other party or something."

"You mean you're not sure if it was Lizbeth you heard talking about the country club this weekend?" Kristen said.

"Well, yeah, I mean, I guess it was Lizbeth. But I think I just misunderstood what she was saying. That happens to me all the time. Ha-ha!" Suddenly I could feel the ol' upper lip sweat as I tried to cover what I'd just done. "I think maybe she was just talking about something her parents were doing, not her. I think that was it," I said again, hoping I sounded convincing.

"Yeah," Kristen said, sharp and clear. "Whatever."

Then she stormed past me back down the hall, clutching her rose purse as if it held the secret weapon she was going to use to destroy her mortal enemy.

I knew I'd blown it. Totally and completely.

Since Kristen was chasing down Lizbeth and Eve wasn't coming, I headed to my usual table with Jonah and Kyle. The two of them were talking about something, some video game probably, and totally ignored me when I sat down. At least, Jonah did. Kyle muttered a meek hello.

"You won't believe what just happened," I said, unpacking the lunch my dad had made me. My hands were still kind of shaking from the conversation with Kristen. "I just opened my big mouth to Kristen about something Lizbeth didn't want her to know. Now she's beyond mad."

"Well, did Lizbeth tell you not to tell anyone?" Jonah asked in this sharp tone of voice that I really wasn't into. I guess it was silly of me to think that he could put aside whatever was bothering him and just be a good friend to me for a minute.

Also, that was a bit of a tricky question. I didn't want to say I was eavesdropping. Which I wasn't. Technically. I just happened to be in the area when I overheard. "She didn't say it was a secret," I said.

He ripped off a bite of his hamburger. He looked

around the caf and said, "Where's your other friend? Eve?"

"She's meeting with her history teacher."

"Why?" he asked.

"Not sure," I said. "He's probably trying to catch her up."

"Well, is she still coming to lunch? She can sit here with us."

"She's not coming. Why do you care?" I asked teasingly.

"You know what?" Jonah said, his face scrunching up.

"Jonah," Kyle said. I'd almost forgotten he was there. "Come on."

"What is wrong with you, Jonah?" I asked. And then I blurted out, "Are you mad at me for hanging out with other people or something?" I realized that sounded kind of catty, but I didn't know what else could possibly be wrong, or why he'd care for two seconds if I had made other friends.

"No! That is not what's wrong with me," he snapped. It made me think that maybe there really was something to it. "And since you've liked sitting at that table so much," he said, nodding over to Lizbeth and Kristen's vacant table, "why don't you just sit there from now on?"

"Jonah, why are you being so mean? Why won't

you tell me what you're angry about?"

"Because," he spat, then stood and picked up his tray. "See you later," he said.

To Kyle.

Wow.

I thought I might start crying. I knew Jonah was angry, but not so angry that he couldn't even tell me *why* he was so angry.

I'd ruined things with Kristen and Lizbeth, and now this. And I still didn't know what I had done!

"It's okay," Kyle said. "He's just in a bad mood."

If I had known things were going to be so wonky today, I would never have gotten out of bed.

CHAPTER 16

Have you ever walked into a room and everyone was acting really weird and you didn't know why but you knew that it had to be something very, very bad? That's what the salon felt like on Wednesday. It had this total off-vibe, like the pomade jar was about to hit the fan.

I was wiping down Mom's mirror when a woman with long red hair came in.

"Janette Williams?" Megan asked, checking the schedule. Great. It was Maggie Williams's mom. I couldn't believe Maggie had actually gotten her mom to come in. I'd forgotten about Maggie and the cell phone promise. Bad vibe or not, I thought something good might be happening when Megan showed Mrs. Williams over to Devon's station. That was, until I figured out what was actually happening.

When Devon come out from the back, ready to cut

and style Mrs. Williams's hair, Mom was right there on her heels.

"Hi there," Devon said to Mrs. Williams. "I'm Devon. Welcome to Hello, Gorgeous!"

"Hello, nice to meet you," Mrs. Williams said, eyeing Mom.

"This is Chloe, owner of the salon." Mom smiled and said a polite hello to Mrs. Williams. Devon wiped her palms on the cute baby duck–print apron she was wearing. "Don't mind her, she's just going to watch what I do here. Nothing to worry about!"

Pretending to be excited was never a good thing. You'd have to be deaf and blind not to know that Devon was worried. Even Mrs. Williams looked like she was wondering what she'd gotten herself into.

Rowan had just walked a client out. "I'll be in my office," she said, referring to her facial room. "No disturbances!" She practically raced back and sealed the door shut.

Giancarlo had just finished up his client. "I'm out of here," he mouthed as he dusted off his chair and peeled out the door.

Piper, who didn't have a client, either, shuffled her apple-red Vans after Giancarlo and whispered, "Don't leave me here!"

Violet cut her eyes at both of them and said, "You guys. Come on." She said it like, *Be cool, relax, and don't make a scene.* Not that Giancarlo or Piper listened to her, salon manager or not. I *so* wanted to leave with them, but there was no way. Unlike the stylists who could leave the premises in between customers, my job required me to be on the floor the whole time. And, also, I had to at least *try* and see if I could squeeze in my Maggie–cell phone pitch at some point. Though with Mom supervising every move Devon made, I didn't know when I'd have the chance.

Here's the deal: Before Mom hires a stylist she doesn't know or who doesn't come personally recommended, she has them cut someone's hair while she watches. It's usually someone who wants a free cut and doesn't mind letting an unknown stylist take a pair of sharp scissors to her head. But never, in all the years Mom had owned the salon, has she had to watch one of her own stylists *after* she'd been hired, as far as I knew, anyway. For Mom to do this to Devon—who supposedly had a lot of experience— meant that things were really bad.

"So," Devon began. "What are we doing today?"

"Well, I like my length up here," Mrs. Williams said, fingering the top of her brassy red hair as Devon and Mom looked at her in the mirror. Mom stood right next to Devon, not even trying to hide the fact that she was watching closely. "I actually want the front layers to grow out a bit, but you can do whatever you want with the rest."

"Okay," Devon said, eyeing Mrs. Williams's hair carefully but glancing over at Mom every few moments or so. "What if it was blunt here . . . ," she said, indicating the sides. Her voice had the slightest quiver to it and it seemed an octave higher than usual. "And we made the back into some piecey layers?"

"Fine by me," she said.

"Great," Devon said. Mrs. Williams was about to get up from her chair to get washed when Mom stepped in.

"Are you sure doing the sides that way is right for her face?" Mom asked. Devon and Mrs. Williams froze on the spot. "She has such a beautiful diamond-shaped face, sharp angles at the sides will give her a cone head look. As beautiful as you are, Janette, I don't think you want that." Mom smiled at her.

"No, thank you," Mrs. Williams said.

"I think something softer on the sides would be better," Mom said to Devon.

Devon's matte red lips pulled into a tight buttonhole, and when she spoke she seemed to calculate each word precisely. "Okay. Sounds good."

Mom finally left Devon's station to let her cut in peace, but Devon would have murdered me if I tried to talk to Mrs. Williams right then. Murdered me or balded me.

Once Devon was finished, Mom inspected Mrs.

Williams's hair with the thoroughness of a teacher grading our year-end tests.

"What's this?" Mom asked, holding pieces of her hair between her fingers. "Uneven." Mom took her own scissors and with one snap made them perfect. She did this in a couple of other places as Devon stood by with her arms wrapped around her waist and her neck turning red.

Mrs. Williams said she liked her cut, which was a good sign, but Mom had to make several adjustments before the final result. When it was over, Mom thanked Mrs. Williams and said she hoped to see her again. Then Mrs. Williams walked out the door, and so did my chance to win the day for Maggie.

"Well," Mom said to Devon. "How do you think you did?"

Devon couldn't even respond. She burst into tears. Mom put her arm around her and guided her back into her office and shut the door. Those of us still on the floor let out a big sigh.

"That was intense," Violet said.

"I wouldn't be able to work if someone was hanging over my shoulder like that, either," Megan said.

"You would if you were talented," Violet said. "I just mean a stylist should be able to work no matter what. You can't lack confidence when you have a pair of scissors in your hands."

Soon Giancarlo and Piper came back with paper cups of CJ's coffee and a bag for me that held a chocolate cupcake. I loved everything from CJ's, but I wasn't sure I could stomach eating just then.

"Where is she?" Piper asked.

"In Mom's office," I said.

"You guys were smart for leaving," Megan said. "It was intense in the worst way."

"Poor Devon," Piper said. "I wonder what the deal is? She came so highly recommended from that fancy place in Boston. Violet talked to the owner herself when we were checking her references."

"I don't know," Giancarlo said. "But she better figure it out quickly or she's out on her can."

A new client walked in, and we all got back into our places, looking like a normal, working salon. I took my cupcake to the break room for later. Mom's door had popped open just enough for me to hear her say, ". . . maybe some classes to sharpen your skills. I can't hold your station forever, but maybe for a few more weeks . . ."

CHAPTER 17

On Thursday, I was getting a sip of water before homeroom; when I finished I almost rammed right into Maggie, who then practically pinned me against the wall. She got so close, I could see a tiny crust of red jam on the corner of her mouth from breakfast.

"Oh my gosh, Mickey!" she said. "My mom was there! How'd it go?"

Please tell me you're kidding. I knew she'd ask me. But she had to know that Cara's mom agreeing to get Cara a cell phone didn't automatically mean Maggie's mom would do the same.

"I, well . . ."

Breathlessly, she began, "I have the perfect phone picked out and all I need is the word from Mom to order it online. I've totally made it easy on her—she doesn't even have to drive me to the mall. So? Tell me! What happened?"

"Well, the thing is," I said. She was so eager I almost couldn't look at her—but she was so up in my business I didn't really have a choice . . .

"I, um, didn't get around to it."

She blinked. "You didn't get around to it? But you promised."

"I didn't promise," I said.

"You totally did."

I was a hundred percent sure I didn't promise, but in that particular moment it didn't seem helpful to tell that to Maggie. "It's just that things were kind of crazy last night and it was never the right time."

"Crazy?" she snipped. She propped her hand on her hip. "What do you mean, *crazy*? Did someone else go bald or something?"

"Someone *else*?"

"You should be thankful I sent my mom there—I totally took a chance. I was practically sacrificing her beautiful hair for you and I get nothing in return? That's so not cool, Mickey."

"Look, I'm sorry. But wait, what do you mean, did someone *else* go bald?"

She stepped back from me and held up a hand. "You can't just make a promise and then not keep it. That's, like, a rule!" She stormed down the hall away from me, her pastel, yellow pleated skirt swishing aggressively as she went.

My day sure was getting off to a terrific start. All I wanted was to know what in the world she was talking about. Who went bald in the first place?

I started toward homeroom, and when I turned the corner I spotted Lizbeth rushing to her own class, her hair flying behind her. We hadn't even been friends for very long and I may have already ruined it. That first day we talked after school was only a couple of weeks ago, the day I gave her and Kristen those stupid nail polishes. The same day I'd told her about Devon and the balding.

Wait a minute . . .

My stomach dropped through the floor.

Could Lizbeth have possibly told people about that—so many that now there was a rumor spreading around town? Could *that* have been the reason Devon wasn't getting any clients? What if all this time it was my fault that Devon's station was empty? How could I live with myself if it was?

On my way out of homeroom, I spotted Kristen in the hall. I took a deep breath and decided to approach her. She was surrounded by a group of friends, which did not include Lizbeth. Normally the two were inseparable. I hoped Lizbeth had just left early for a doctor's appointment or was in a different part of school just then.

"Hey, Kristen," I said. I wasn't sure why I was so

nervous. After all, I hadn't done anything wrong to her. "I'm sure you already have plans but, um, if you want, I'm probably going to sit with Eve at lunch today. Do you want us to save a seat for you?"

A faint smile crossed Kristen's face. "I'll see you guys later, okay?" she said to the girls, who nodded and walked away. "Thanks, Mickey. That's very nice. But I'm not really in the mood. I think I'm going to go hide out in the nurse's office, fake some stomach cramps or something."

"Are you sure?" I said. "You have to eat."

"Yeah, well . . . I guess I'm not really up for mystery meat or whatever else they might be serving." She added a little giggle at the end, but it was obvious how sad she felt.

"I'm sorry," I said, and I think she understood exactly what I meant.

"Thanks for asking, though," she said before heading toward the nurse's office.

I met Eve right outside the cafeteria and as soon as we walked inside, she made a beeline for Jonah's table, which I wasn't expecting. I wasn't sure how Jonah would feel about me sitting at his table, but by that point, it would have been pretty awkward for me to try and get Eve to sit anywhere else.

Eve chattered away about English class while we

ate. Kyle never talked, Jonah was sulking—he wouldn't even look at me—and I couldn't stop thinking about Kristen and Lizbeth.

"What do you think, Mickey?" Eve asked, breaking into my thoughts. "You think Ms. Carlisle is going to make us do a report on it?"

"Oh, um, yeah. Probably." I had no idea what *it* was because I was off in Obsessoland. I shot a look at Jonah, but he took one last bite of burrito, dropped the rest on his lunch tray, and stood up.

"See you guys later," he mumbled.

"Hey, wait," I said, and he grudgingly looked back at me. "Where're you going?"

"I'm done," he said.

For a moment, it looked like Jonah was going to say something else. Instead, he grabbed a napkin off the table, crumpled it on his tray, and muttered a good-bye.

"Bye, Jonah!" Eve said, trying to sound chipper.

If Jonah kept running away every time we came within two feet of each other, then how in the world was I ever going to get him to tell me what he was so angry about?

Right after lunch I spotted Lizbeth coming out of the library and all my Jonah worries gave way to my Lizbeth worries. I wondered if she had eaten in there alone.

I *so* didn't want to talk to her. Well, I *wanted* to talk to her, but not about what I had to talk to her about. I sucked it up and approached her, anyway.

"Hi, Lizbeth," I said, trying to act like everything was fine. "How's it going?"

Her light brown eyes cut through me with such intensity they seemed lit from behind like a demon's in a horror movie.

"Are you seriously talking to me?"

Panic rose inside me. I knew she'd be upset—but I didn't know how to handle it, so I tried to play dumb. "Um . . . yeah? I mean, are you and Kristen fighting?"

"No, we're not," she snapped. "We're not even talking. At all. The fight is over and so is our friendship. So thanks a lot for opening your big mouth to her about the fund-raiser. What were you—eavesdropping the whole time or something?"

"No, I mean, I'm sorry, but I—"

"And what was that whole thing with the nail polish? Did you steal those?"

"Of course not!" I protested. *Because taking and stealing are totally different.* My stomach clenched at the mention of them, though.

"Because I didn't ask you to do that," she pointed out.

"I know, it's not a big deal, really."

"Whatever." Her voice quivered, and I could tell she was trying to get away from me, but I couldn't let her go without at least finding out about Devon. Maybe I could fix one messy situation in the thousands I had racked up. "Look, I'm really sorry about you and Kristen. I honestly am. I'll talk to her if you want me to—"

"Don't even."

"Okay. I won't talk to her," I said, speaking as quickly as I could so I could cram in my Devon question before she got away from me. "Listen . . . I know you want me to leave you alone, but there's something I have to ask you. Did you say anything to anyone about Devon? Like, about what kind of stylist she is? Because things are really bad for her at the salon and I was just wondering if, you know, you told anyone that story I told you about her."

Lizbeth put her hand on her hip in a very snotty way that made me nervous. "First of all," she began, "yeah, I told some people about her making people go bald. Why shouldn't I have? Your mom shouldn't even have someone like that working there."

"You don't understand—I'm not even sure that story was true."

"Oh, great—now you're a liar and a thief!" she said.

How could I explain that I'd only done all these

things because I wanted her to like me? It was so pathetic, I almost couldn't stand it.

"Also, just so we're straight," she continued, "whether or not I invite Kristen on Saturday is none of your business."

"I know it's not my business. I only said something because . . . I just assumed she'd be going!" I said.

"Yeah, well, you shouldn't assume things about people you don't even know. Kristen either steals away attention from every guy I've ever liked or she makes a fool of me the way she did with Matthew at the game. Why would I want to deal with *that* at the fund-raiser?"

With that, Lizbeth pushed past me and stomped down the hall more upset than ever. I couldn't believe what was happening. Everyone was miserable and unhappy. And it was all my fault. I just wanted to go back to being the girl who got people cell phones and gave everyone a heads-up on pop quizzes, not the girl who spread rumors that weren't true, got people fired, and broke up best friends.

I had to figure out a way to make it all go away before everyone hated me for life—and also before Mom found out.

CHAPTER 18

As I finished getting ready Saturday morning (aka frying my hair with a curling iron and then shoving the whole mess into a ponytail holder), I looked out my bedroom window to see what Jonah was up to. I could see a flash of boy leg in the living room—no doubt it was him playing Warpath.

I crossed the backyard and started into the house from the back door, doing my usual two knocks followed by letting myself in. Only this time, after I knocked, I turned the handle and found that the door was locked. I was sure Jonah was home, so I knocked again. After a moment, the door opened.

"Hi, Mickey," Mrs. Goldman said.

"Oh, hi. Is Jonah here?"

"Well," she said, looking over her shoulder. "I'm afraid he's not available, sweetie."

Not available? I couldn't believe my ears. Jonah

must have told his mother not to let me in. And she hadn't tried to talk him out of it, which meant she agreed with his reasons, whatever they were. "Oh," I managed to say. "Okay. Well, could you just tell him I came by? To see what's up?"

"Of course, Mickey," she said. "I'll tell him."

I felt so hurt I practically had to drag myself to the salon.

"There's no spring to that step," Megan said when I got to Hello, Gorgeous!

"What's there to spring about?" I asked.

It was a regular Saturday with a steady flow of customers, the phone ringing every ten seconds and the sound of Giancarlo's laughter floating through the salon. I carried a stack of fresh towels to the sinks and then went to the front to see if Megan needed anything.

"Want to grab a diet and a regular?" Megan asked as two women took a seat in the lounge. She had the phone in the crook of her neck and greeted a third woman as she came in the door.

I got the drinks, opened them carefully, and handed them to the women.

"Katie?" Megan said, hanging up the phone and looking at a slim woman in capris and wedges. "Piper is about ready for you. She'll be up in one sec."

"I'll show her to the changing room if you want," I said.

"You're a lifesaver, Mick," Megan said.

I smiled at the woman in the lounge. "Katie? Right this way." We walked through the thick of the salon chaos. Giancarlo almost ran over us carrying back an extra dish of dye, and Piper carried a section of brunette hair extensions that fluttered behind her like streamers. "Some days I feel like I'm in a real-life video game, dodging stylists to get through this craziness."

Katie laughed and said, "Yeah, it's insane here today."

I shrugged. "It's always this crazy on Saturdays." I opened the dressing room door. "Right in here. Piper should be ready when you get out."

"Thank you," she said.

The only part of the salon that wasn't crazy was Devon's station. Even Devon herself seemed to have abandoned ship, leaving her station stylist-less.

I found her in the break room when I went back to take my own break. She sat staring at the wall across from her, gnawing on an apple slice. Her short black hair was as straight and shiny as ever, but she wore all black—baggy cargos and an equally baggy top—and not a single splash of color.

"Hey, Devon," I said, getting my bag from the

shelf. I dug out the turkey with provolone wrap Dad had packed for me and set it on the table.

"Hey," she said, not moving her eyes from the wall. She put the half-eaten apple slice on the plastic bag in front of her, barely moving.

"Are you okay?" I asked.

She turned her eyes toward me as if finally realizing I was there. She sat up straight and took a big, deep breath. "I'm fine," she said, even though she clearly didn't look it.

My heart raced, and I knew I had to ask her about her old salon. The problem was, she was so down and depressed, I worried that anything we talked about could make things worse. Knowing it was all because of me made me feel awful, but it also gave me the determination to do something about it. "So, like . . ." I began as delicately as I could given what I was about to ask her. "About your last salon in Boston. What was that like?"

She shrugged one shoulder. "Nice. On Newbury Street, so we had high-end clients. Impossible to get an appointment. Always busy, like here. Well." She gave a hiccup of a laugh. "For some stylists."

I pulled the tinfoil off the wrap, then closed it back up. The idea of eating didn't seem so great just then. "What happened there?"

Without looking at me she said, "What do you mean?"

"Well, you said something once about, um, a balding incident?"

Devon looked at me blankly, her mouth hanging open slightly. "What are you talking about?"

"Some client of yours went bald? Because of a cut you gave her?"

Devon pulled her head back in exasperation. "You think I made someone go bald? Are you crazy?"

My stomach cramped up and just having food near me made me want to gag. I pushed the wrap away from me. "I thought I heard you say something. Like, there was some accident or something?"

She shook her head furiously. "No, I once buzzed a girl's hair marine-short, but that's because she asked me to do it. She wanted to freak out her mom and it worked. She loved me. But it wasn't an accident at all." Devon bore her eyes into me and asked, "Mickey, why are you asking this? Has someone been saying things about me?"

I shook my head no, scooting away from the table and pulling myself up. I kept my hand on the arm of the chair to help steady myself. Devon stood up with me, as if she was going to block my way out of the break room.

"No," I said. "Not that I know of."

"Are you sure about that?"

I nodded my head, but she wasn't buying it.

"Something's going on and I want to know what it is."

Those pesky beads of sweat started to form on my upper lip. I swallowed hard. "Nothing's going on."

Devon fixed her green eyes on me and folded her arms across her chest. "I have no clients, no one seems to know why, and now you're asking me about making a woman go bald? Kid, you better spill it and spill it quick."

"It's nothing," I said, feeling desperate.

"Nothing, huh? You think I don't know about those nail polishes?" My heart raced and I felt like the breath was being sucked out of me. I was so going to faint before this was over. "Violet's inventory is never off, and she does it every week so I knew it wasn't a simple mix-up. Then I caught what was going on with you and your little friend last weekend and that green polish. One of the exact ones Karen's been looking for?"

"I'm going to tell my mom about it," I said quickly. "Tonight. I'm telling her."

"Or I could tell her right now, unless you start talking. I'm serious, Mickey. This is my job we're talking about."

I wanted to cry. Bawl is more like it. Shoulders shaking, hyperventilating, dehydration setting in—that sort of thing. Somehow I managed to keep the tears away for the moment. The rest of it, though, came spilling out of my mouth.

"Well I overheard you saying that one time you made that client of yours in Boston go bald, and I guess I misunderstood and thought you didn't do it on purpose and then I told someone who might have told a couple more people and then suddenly no one would let you do their hair and I guess it's because they all thought you made women go bald and I'm so, so sorry, Devon. Really, I promise, I am."

I took a breath and watched the realization slowly seep into her expression. Her eyes widened and her mouth puckered.

"*You?*" she began. "I've been practically clientless because of *you*? That client of mine *wanted* me to shave her head."

"I know!"

"I'm a great stylist!" she said.

"I'm so sorry. Honestly."

Devon stared me down. Hours passed before she said, "What are you going to do about it?"

Gulp.

"I'll fix it."

"How?"

I could hear Giancarlo laughing out on the floor, and thought how lucky he was to be so carefree at the very moment I was sinking into great failure.

"I'll think of something. I promise," I said, even though I had zero idea what I could do.

She picked up another apple slice and snapped off a bite. "You have until tomorrow, or I'm going to your mother and telling her exactly why I haven't had any clients," she said. "I can't afford to have my chair empty any longer."

"Don't worry," I said.

Don't worry? What had I gotten myself into? What was I going to do?

As stressed as I was, and horrified at what I had done, I knew I had to go talk to Mom before I did anything else. Not just because Devon had threatened to rat me out, but because it was time for me to start fixing my mistakes. This conversation was long overdue.

I knocked on her office door before opening it. She stood behind her desk putting papers in a folder, looking the opposite of how I felt—she was totally put together in skinny dark denim jeans and a black top with a gold belt.

"Hi, honey," Mom said. "Is my two o'clock here?"

"I'm not sure. I just finished my break."

She checked her makeup in the compact on her desk. "Everything okay out there?"

"Yes," I said, my voice giving the tiniest quiver.

"Honey?" Mom said, setting down the compact.

She took a step toward me and said, "Are you okay? You look a little flushed."

I couldn't take it anymore. I spilled it all out as fast as I could, just to be rid of it. "*I* took the other bottles of those new polishes. Peppermint Shake and Cornflower Blues. I'm sorry. I gave them to some girls at school because they liked them so much and I know I shouldn't have taken them without asking or paying or anything and I swear I won't do it again or anything like it." I could have kept the momentum going and told her about Devon, too, but something held me back. Maybe because I thought I could fix it on my own. And maybe a little because I was afraid my mother would kill me. "Am I fired?"

Mom looked stunned for a second but quickly recovered, taking a deep breath. "I knew that Violet's inventory reports are never wrong, so something had to be off—something inside the salon. Did you know that for a moment I thought Devon might have taken them? Because she's the only new person here—besides you."

"It wasn't Devon."

"How could you do such a thing? I'm so disappointed in you."

Tears welled up in my eyes as I said, "I'm so sorry. I thought the bottles Karen had would be enough, but I guess deep down I knew that still wouldn't make taking them okay. I just wanted those girls to like me."

The angry lines in my mother's face softened. "Honey, you don't need to give people things in order to make them like you—you know that. They'll just like you for who you are."

I started to sob. *If only that was true.*

Mom put her arms around me and the sobs turned to heaves. We just stood there in an embrace for a while. Eventually, I calmed down.

"I'm sorry things have been so difficult for you lately," she said. Then she let go of me and looked me straight in the eye.

I sensed that Sensitive and Understanding Mom was about to shift into Strict and Tough Mom.

"Is there anything else you want to tell me?"

I kept my eyes on the floor. There was no way she knew about the Devon situation. Even I'd only just found out. And as bad as it was, it was something I really wanted to fix myself, if I could just figure out a way how. If I couldn't fix it, then I really didn't deserve to work at the salon—not even if I worked for free.

I shook my head. "No. There's nothing else."

Mom took a deep breath and looked me square in the eyes. "Mickey, I need you to leave the salon for the rest of the day. You need to think about what you've done. I'm working late tonight, so we'll talk more at breakfast tomorrow and see if there's still a place for you here. Do you understand me?"

"Yes," I managed as the tears came spilling out again.

On my walk home, the sun was shining and the birds were chirping, but I couldn't have cared less. All I could think about was how many things I had to set right. I'd done a lot of damage; now it was time to start cleaning it up.

CHAPTER 19

I'd like to say that as soon as I got home I started thinking up a plan that would save my spot at the salon as well as save Devon from the rumor I'd apparently started. But I didn't. I went home, collapsed on my bed, and started bawling.

I didn't know what I was going to do. Everything I had wanted to change in my life, everything I'd wanted to become, I'd totally ruined. I felt like I'd gotten a taste of what it was like to work at the salon and have girlfriends, and as soon as I got used to it, it was taken away. By me. Because I had no one to blame but myself.

I looked out across our backyard from my bedroom window. I spotted Jonah's legs again.

This was totally ridiculous. He couldn't avoid me forever, and I couldn't stand not knowing what, exactly, I'd done to make him so upset.

I knocked twice on the back door and this time when I tried the handle, it wasn't locked. And with no one to stop me, I walked into the living room, as if nothing was wrong. "Hey."

Jonah looked over at me, and something exploded on the TV.

"Great, thanks a lot," he said as a GAME OVER screen came up.

"What is that?" I asked, not recognizing the outer space and alien graphics.

"You should know," Jonah said. He tossed the controller to the floor in front of him. He got up off the floor and plopped himself on the couch. I sat myself down on the opposite end.

"How should I know?" I asked carefully. He didn't even look at me. I heard the whine in my voice when I asked, "Why are you so mad at me?"

"Shouldn't you be at a *friend's* house or something?"

My eyes welled up once again. He had no idea how much that stung. "Look, Jonah. Whatever's wrong, whatever I did, I'm sorry. Okay? Please, *please* don't be mad at me because everyone else is."

He shrugged. "Maybe you deserve to have everyone mad at you."

Okay. *Cold.*

"That's it—tell me what I did. I can't take it

anymore. Are you mad because I've been hanging out with the girls lately?"

With every second that passed, it was harder and harder to hold back my tears. Finally, one slipped past the goalie and down my cheek. I quickly brushed it away. I don't think I'd ever felt so alone and rejected in my whole life.

"Do you seriously think I'd be mad at you because of *them*?" Jonah asked.

"I don't know!" I shrieked as the tears rushed down my cheek. "I have no idea why you're mad at me!"

He shifted on the couch to face me more fully. "I'm mad because, first of all, you totally bailed on me. You said you would come to the store with my dad and me after school last Thursday and then back here to help me break in the new Warpath of Doom." He shoved his finger toward the TV, still displaying GAME OVER. "And then you just didn't show. No word, no explanation, nothing. And then for the last week you've been acting like you're suddenly ashamed of me, wanting nothing to do with me whenever your wonderful new friends come along, like you're embarrassed to be in the same zip code as me. *That's* why I'm mad. Now you can leave."

I cringed. I'd totally forgotten that I'd promised to come over on Thursday. I'd been so wrapped up with going to the baseball game with Lizbeth and Kristen that Jonah and Warpath flew right out of my head.

"Jonah, I'm so sorry. You're right—you should be mad at me. I've been terrible. Thursday completely slipped my mind." I took a deep breath, trying to keep more tears away. "I don't have an excuse for how I've been treating you. I guess I thought you'd somehow embarrass me in front of the girls and then they wouldn't like me anymore. I know it's stupid, but . . . that was pretty much how I was thinking."

"How would I embarrass you?" he asked. As soon as I heard the words come out of my mouth, I knew I was just digging myself into a deeper hole. His face reddened at the prospect of having an added reason to be angry at me.

"That came out wrong," I said, hoping to take the sting out of it. "I guess I was just worried that you'd burp the whole alphabet or make underarm farts or something like that, and they'd think I like that kind of thing."

Thank goodness, that made him laugh. "First of all, anyone who doesn't appreciate the ancient art of underarm farts isn't worth being friends with in the first place, and, second of all, if they didn't like you because they didn't like me, *that'd* be pretty stupid."

I managed a small smile. "I know. You're right. Jonah, I'm *so* sorry. I really am. I hope you don't hate me forever."

He aimed the remote at the TV and turned it off game mode and started flipping through the channels. "I don't hate you. Just don't act like that around me again. Like, ever. It was so not cool."

"I won't, I promise. I'm really sorry, about everything."

He started to smile and said, "I guess I can forgive you, then."

I started to breathe normally again. "Thanks, Jonah."

"Whatever," he said with a crooked smile on his face.

I wanted to talk to him about what was happening with Lizbeth, Kristen, Devon, and the stolen polishes, but it felt like a bit much after just making up. I didn't want him to think I only came over so I could dump my problems on him. Besides, taking a break from the drama to watch *Deadliest Catch* seemed like the perfect thing to do just then. We settled into the couch and watched as one of the boats made an emergency stop at Dutch Harbor. At the commercial Jonah said, without looking at me, "What happened to . . ." and he motioned to the top of his head. He meant my hair.

I cringed. "I know."

"I know I'm a guy and everything, and I say this as a friend," Jonah said. "But your hair really is jacked."

For some reason, while the crew on TV was dumping crab pots into the Bering Sea, I decided to take out my ponytail holder and see what happened if I let my hair go wild. This was obviously a mistake. On the up side, Jonah had called me his friend.

"It's a lost cause," I said. "I've had it all my life and I still don't know how to fix it."

"Didn't you like it the day you got that makeover when you first started?"

"Yeah."

"So do it like that."

I rolled my eyes. "I would if I could, obviously. I can never make it look as good as the stylists do. No one can."

"Maybe you should ask someone there to help you, then. They're all pros and you see them every week. I'm sure someone there could you give you a lesson or something."

He had a good point. If there was just some way for all the stylists to help hopeless cases like me do their own hair, then the town would be so happy—not to mention a little bit more gorgeous.

We watched two more episodes of *Deadliest Catch* before I walked back home. As I brushed my hair getting ready for bed, I thought about how right Jonah was when he said I should get the stylists to show me how to fix my hair. The only problem was, they were always too busy working on paying customers to stop and help me with styling. Plus, they'd already styled me for free on my birthday—I couldn't ask them to do it again.

As I climbed into bed, I realized that actually, there was one person at the salon who wasn't that busy, not at all.

Someone, in fact, who was desperate for a little work.

CHAPTER 20

The next morning I woke up to my alarm screaming at me. It was 8:30. On a normal Sunday I would have been getting up to dress for the salon. This morning, though, I wasn't sure if I was ever going to be allowed back.

I showered and dressed as if I would be. Figured I might as well be positive about the whole thing. I dressed in a tie-dyed tank with a pinstripe vest and black jeans, then headed downstairs, ready to face what happened next.

Sort of.

Mom sat sipping coffee while Dad served up hot blueberry muffins in his navy apron.

"Good morning, Mikaela," Mom said. That's when I knew the news would not be good.

"Morning," I said, slipping into the chair.

"Fresh muffin?" Dad asked, holding a muffin pan

in his oven-mitted hand.

"Sure," I said. "Thanks."

Mom took a sip of her coffee, then asked, "How did it feel, being sent home yesterday?"

"Awful," I said.

"Mickey, I really can't emphasize enough how inappropriate—how *wrong* it was of you, taking those polishes without asking."

"I know," I said. "I promise I'll never do it again."

"Since you can't ask for them back, you'll have to pay for them with your own money."

Seemed fair enough.

"You're not going to work with me today, either. I want you to stay home and help Dad with the chores."

I wasn't sure what to do. I *had* to get to the salon to talk to Devon about the idea I had last night. My time was running out. I'd just have to tell Dad I was going for a walk, then go to the salon and somehow talk to her without Mom seeing me. I had no idea how I'd manage that, but I had to make it work.

"And you're not to leave the house today," Mom continued. "Or for the rest of the week, aside from school and the salon—if I decide you can go back on Wednesday."

Well, there went talking to Devon. In person any way. I'd have to call her. Maybe in the early evening when things got quieter and the noise of the blow-dryers died down.

"I hope you're ready for some manual labor." Dad grinned, taking off his apron and sitting down with us. "We've got yard work to do!" I set my muffin back on my plate, my appetite gone. "Come on! It's good for your soul."

I tried not to groan. The last time I helped my dad with yard work, I accidentally dug into an ant hill. The ants swarmed over my legs in two seconds flat, and I swear the queen herself tried to attack me.

Mom finished up her breakfast and kissed me on the head before she left. Dad and I put away the dishes, and when we finished he looked at me and said, "Unless you think dirt goes with that outfit, I suggest you change. We've got a messy job ahead of us."

It was going to be a *long* day.

After hours of pulling weeds, planting a few flowers, and being attacked by *several* beetles, I took my second shower of the day and put on my pajamas. It was so early, it was still light out, but I didn't care.

Once I was in my pajamas, there really was nothing left for me to do except to call Devon. I prayed that she would like the idea I came up with. Otherwise, I'd have to kiss Hello, Gorgeous! good-bye.

"Hello, Gorgeous!" Megan's sunny voice cheered when she answered the phone.

My stomach was in knots. "Uh . . .," I began, my voice lowered as much as I could to disguise it. "Devon, please." Why didn't I have her cell number so I could have called her directly? Less than a minute passed before Megan got her.

"Devon? Hey, it's Mickey." Silence on the other end. "Hello?"

"I'm here," she said. "Why aren't you?"

"I've been suspended. Because of the nail polish thing." For some odd, brief moment I thought she might say something sympathetic to me. But, no . . . not a chance. Just a grunt from her end of the line. "Um, anyway, that's why I'm calling. Because I can't come in and tell you my idea."

"Tell me now," she said. "I'm dying to know."

Dying—she sounded more like she was ready for murder.

So I started to explain my half-baked idea of showing people how to style their own hair, like the pros do. That way, the day after a great cut and style, women would be able to do their own hair and look just as gorgeous the second day as when they walked out of the salon.

"We can use regular people as models, like maybe girls from my school for the demonstrations. And then, the people you style will probably love what you do and they'll probably become regulars and then tell all their friends and then you'll have a ton of clients. So, yeah. Um, I think people would really like it."

She didn't make a sound the entire time I rambled. I had no idea if she was liking the idea or if she thought it blew.

Finally, I heard her let out a breath. Then I heard her voice. It took a minute for me to make sense of her words: "I think this could work."

I was so relieved I wanted to dive through the phone and hug her.

"On one condition," she continued. "You have to let me cut your hair."

That word. *Cut.* I was hoping she wouldn't use it. Suddenly I was seeing *bangs* in my future. Or worse.

"Do you *have* to cut it? I asked. "I mean, this is just a styling thing, not a cutting thing. I think it'd be weird to cut my hair, too, don't you think? I think it might be." *Voodoo mind tricks,* I thought. *Make her believe you.*

"In order to style your hair well, it needs a good cut as a foundation. So yes, I do have to cut it."

"But no bangs or anything crazy like that, right?" I asked, adding in a laugh for effect. *Ha, ha, ha!* As if that was the ca-raziest idea ever invented.

I could practically hear the face she was making at me through the phone. "Listen, you want to do this idea of yours, you let me cut your hair. Simple."

If I wanted to keep my job at Hello, Gorgeous!, I had to go along with her plan. It was either risk my hair or lose my job.

As I told her I'd do it, I had visions of my hair falling strand by strand to the floor as Devon laughed a menacing laugh.

"Excellent," she said. "I'll go talk to your mom about it. And since it's such a great idea, I'm gonna act like it was all mine. Sound good?"

"Sounds great," I said, and we hung up. It wasn't like I had much choice now, was it?

I didn't sleep much at all that night.

But the next day, at least one thing was back to normal—Jonah came in through our back door to walk with me to school.

"Nice of you to show," I joked.

"Watch it, or I won't let you sit with me at lunch."

"Let me?" I said. "You'd be lucky if I decided I wanted to."

But I did.

I spotted Eve coming out of the office before homeroom.

"Hey!" I said. "Wait up." I ran and caught up with her.

"Hi," she said. "What's going on?"

"Everything okay?" I asked, nodding to the office.

"Yeah. I just have to have all this stuff from my old school transferred and it's been a pain. Plus I've had to spend some lunches working with my teachers to get caught up on things they didn't cover at my old school. But now I think I'm done and can finally be a regular student."

"Ha, lucky you," I said. We started walking down the hall. "Do you want to sit with me and Jonah at lunch today?"

"Sure," she said.

And then I just blurted it out. "Do you like Jonah?" I asked, and, unlike me, I could tell she knew I meant *like* like.

"He's kind of cute," she said in a half-whisper.

"Eve!" I said. "I can't believe it!" Even though I totally could—the clues had been there all along.

"But please don't tell him, okay?" she said. "I don't want to make a big deal about it, especially since I just got to this school."

"Okay," I said. "I won't."

This time, I really *would* keep my mouth shut. There was no way I'd ever make the mistake of blabbing again.

Later, when lunch came around, I stood outside the caf waiting for Eve. When she didn't show up, I looked around inside for her and saw that she was already sitting with Jonah. I wished I could be as bold as she was. Maybe one day I would be.

I spotted Kristen sitting with a group of girls. At least she was back to eating in the cafeteria. I didn't see Lizbeth anywhere, though. I wondered if she was still eating in the library. When I sat down, Jonah and Eve were arguing over which ride at Six Flags New England was the scariest.

"That ride can't even touch Mind Eraser," Jonah said. "You're practically dangling off your seat, and it loops and loops you around at, like, the speed of an Indy race car!"

"Please," Eve said. "Catapult all the way. It feels like you're flying right up to the sky, and then just when you're sure you can reach out and touch a cloud, *bam*! You're jerked back down."

"Big deal," Jonah said. "I'm talking about roller coasters. Not kid rides."

No wonder Eve liked Jonah. The two of them were exactly alike. When they noticed me sit down, Jonah snickered, "Mickey almost wet herself on the Mind Eraser two years ago."

"Ugh, so not true," I said. "I was just worried about my cute new sandals falling off," I told Eve. Jonah made a noise that we ignored.

"I like the classic wooden coasters," Kyle said. He blushed when we all turned to look at him. "Thunderbolt all the way."

I nodded. "Yeah, that's a good one." Kyle never said much, but he was kind of cute when he did.

"Where are Kristen and Lizbeth?" Eve asked. "I thought you guys were all friends."

"You've missed a lot," I said, turning away from Kyle who was once again looking closely at his sandwich.

"Well, talk fast, then."

I told her, Jonah, and Kyle how what'd I'd said to Kristen about going to the fund-raiser this weekend had set off a major fight between her and Lizbeth, and with me and Lizbeth. "She won't even talk to me," I said. "And that's not all," I continued. "I have another huge problem." I told them about the Devon rumor.

"Wow," Eve said. "You've been busy."

Jonah looked at me and said, "Seriously. Why didn't you tell me any of this last night?"

I shrugged. "It didn't seem like the right time."

Jonah rolled his eyes. "I'm your friend, okay?" Which I think meant any time is the right time, and I was grateful to him for saying so.

"Okay," I said. "Thanks. I actually do have an idea for Devon, though," I said. "Inspired by you."

"Oh, yeah?" he asked.

"Totally. From last night, at your house when you said my hair looked terrible."

"Nice going, Goldman," Eve said.

"No, it's okay," I said. Then I told them my idea.

"I would totally go to that," Eve said. (Even though, as I learned early on, she's *already* a whiz at styling her own hair.)

"I like the idea, too," Kyle said, out of nowhere.

"Kyle," I said, "you don't say much, but when you do, it's pure genius." He blushed.

"Mickey, you are so lucky you get to work at a salon," Eve said. "You get to be there with all that glam and you totally don't make a big deal about it. If I worked there I'd be using all the products and showing off about what a great job I have."

I *was* lucky. But I was also angry at myself for letting things go so wrong.

When I didn't say anything, Eve said, "I didn't mean that to sound like I was asking for anything. Oh my gosh, did it sound like I was digging for a freebie? Because I totally wasn't, I swear."

"Nice going, Eve," Jonah laughed. "Why don't you just ask her to give you the works while you're at it?"

"Watch it, boy," she said. "Because I'm this close to going Sergeant Sniper on you."

That shut Jonah up. "That's from level seven of Warpath of Doom. How do you know about him?"

Eve grinned. "Because I rule that game, that's how."

As they started arguing-slash-talking about the

video game, I thought about the two of them as a couple and if that'd be weird for me. I quickly decided I didn't care, as long as they were nice to each other.

I realized that if I hadn't been working at the salon, Jonah and Eve might never have become friends. Sure, they'd each still be going to the same school, but our grade is so big, they might never have noticed each other if they hadn't seen each other at the salon first.

And there's no way I would have ever spoken to Lizbeth and Kristen if I hadn't met them at the salon.

Since Hello, Gorgeous! had done such good things for me, maybe it could also help put things right between Lizbeth and Kristen again.

But how?

CHAPTER 21

Tuesday evening, Mom came into my room as I was getting ready for bed. She sat on the edge of my bed while I brushed my hair at my vanity.

"Tomorrow's Wednesday," she said. "Do you think you're ready to go back to the salon?"

"Yes, totally," I said, setting down my brush.

Mom nodded her head thoughtfully. "Okay. But, Mickey, I can't stress enough . . ."

"I know, Mom," I said. She raised an eyebrow at my interrupting her. "I just mean that I know what a huge mistake I made and I promise I won't ever do it or anything like it again."

She kept her eyes on me, considering. Then she reached across and patted my leg before standing up. "Okay. But I'm watching."

When I walked into the salon on Wednesday,

Megan gave me a cheery hello, which always helped brighten my day. She looked beautiful in a bubble skirt with a scoop-necked top and her hair slicked back in a shiny ponytail.

"Hey! Welcome back!" she said. "You feeling better?"

"Huh?" I asked.

"Your mom said you left early on Saturday and didn't work on Sunday because you had some stomach bug."

I had to admit—covering for me like that was a supercool mom move.

"Oh, yeah," I said. "Much better, thanks."

I looked around the salon. Devon usually worked on Wednesdays, but I didn't see her. Giancarlo was working on a man in his twenties, spiking up his hair in the front, and Violet and Piper were also working on clients—sisters, actually, who drove down from Vermont twice a year for a cut and color.

"Is Devon here?" I asked.

"In the break room."

I went to the back to stash my bag, sticking my head in Mom's office to let her know I was there.

"Welcome back," she said with a look in her eyes that seemed to say, *Now don't screw it up*.

Devon was in the back reading a magazine.

"So you've decided to come back to the scene of the crime, huh?" she said. I think she was making a joke, but I wasn't sure.

"Uh, yeah," I said, way too nervous to think of a snappy comeback.

"I talked to your mom about your idea," she continued. "You're in luck. She loves it."

"Seriously?"

"Yep. And she wants to start on it this coming Saturday."

Devon said that after Mom agreed, word spread quickly to the other stylists, who were all eager to help out. Devon's problem—created by yours truly—had let a bad vibe seep into the salon. Everyone was anxious to be a happy Hello, Gorgeous! family once again.

"Hey, Mick . . . that's pretty exciting about Be Gorgeous, huh?" Piper said to me as soon as I got out on the floor. "Hey, Chloe," she said to Mom as she walked up to reception. "I got the DJ at KBRK to do some on-air promos to drive in customers. Cool, huh?"

"Nice work, Piper," Mom said.

"Make sure he mentions that the owner's daughter is the first one up," Devon said with a sly eye toward me. "That should intrigue people."

"Totally," Piper said. "I mean, you have to be a pretty good stylist to work on the owner's daughter, right?"

"That's the idea," Devon said, and a shiver went down my spine.

"Thanks, honey, for agreeing to help out Devon," Mom said, resting her hand on my shoulder blade. "That's very sweet of you." She clearly didn't see the looks that passed between me and Devon.

"She just wants her hair done for free," Piper joked. I forced a smile and a laugh to show that—*gulp*—I was totally fine with the idea of Devon getting near my hair.

As I was leaving for the day, I passed the small room where Rowan was giving facials to two women. They looked like they were morphing into sea creatures with their faces covered in light green paste and cucumbers over their eyes. They had left the tan curtain that separated the two sections open, talking away without seeing each other. Their hands moved in gestures, with one even reaching out for the other through cucumber blindness to make a point.

I sat in the lounge area waiting as Megan straightened up her desk. She took a wet cloth and wiped down the drawing fishbowl.

Seeing the bowl reminded me of something.

Lizbeth had dropped two cards in for a drawing. One for herself and one for Kristen.

The time had come for Lizbeth and Kristen to win that drawing.

CHAPTER 22

On my way out of the salon that evening, I stepped into Mom's office to ask for a favor. It probably wasn't the best time to be asking her to do something for me, but, hey, a friendship was on the line.

"Hey, Mom?" I said, stepping into her office. "Do you think it'd be okay if I worked Friday night? I don't have any plans and I just want to get back into the swing of things here."

She sat back in her chair, thinking. After a moment, as if she couldn't find a reason why not, she said, "I suppose."

Back at reception I bought two gift certificates for facials.

I got my wallet out of my bag, which held nothing but a video rental card I'd never used, some pictures of my family that I never thought to look at, and a cracked/smashed peppermint hard candy. I opened

195

my wallet. I had some cash in it from my first pay period, but not nearly as much as I needed.

"I'm back on Friday," I told Megan. "Can I bring it to you then? You know I'm good for it."

"Of course," Megan said. "Want two envelopes?"

"Actually, can you hold them here? Under the names Lizbeth Ballinger and Kristen Campbell."

"Sure thing."

"And is Rowan free Friday afternoon? For facials, one at four o'clock and another at four thirty?"

Megan checked the schedule and said she was free. I asked her to schedule Kristen and Lizbeth, respectively, and she did.

"Whatever you're up to seems like a nice surprise," she said as she typed the girls' names into the schedule.

At home, while Dad made pasta sauce for dinner, I went into the office with the computer. I turned it on and clicked on the icon for Mom's salon e-mail account, which was right on the desktop. I checked the school directory and typed out two e-mails: one to Lizbeth and another to Kristen, congratulating them on winning our in-store drawing. I typed that their prize was a gift certificate for a facial, good on one day and at one time only: Friday afternoon for both of them, one scheduled for four o'clock and the other for four fifteen.

On the bottom of the e-mails I added a line that

said: *Do not reply to this e-mail. If for any reason you cannot make this appointment you need not let us know. Again, offer is only valid at the specific date and time given above.* I did this so that they wouldn't write back or call and accidentally tip off my mom to my plan. It was a little risky, but so was doing nothing. And if I knew anything at all about these two girls, I knew they weren't about to give up free facials.

I heard Mom's car pull into the driveway just as I sent the e-mails. I quickly shut off the monitor and left the office, saying a silent prayer that my scheme would work.

Down at the dinner table, Dad served up ziti and Mom unwrapped a fresh baguette she'd picked up at CJ's.

"Don't say I never contribute to dinner." She dropped the baguette on the long bread plate in the center of the table.

"How was work, girls?" Dad asked, serving himself up a steamy pile of ziti.

"Actually," Mom began, cracking off the end of the baguette, "since Devon came up with the idea for Be Gorgeous, the whole mood at the salon has changed."

"Oh yeah?" Dad asked. I guess Mom had already told him about the demonstration, which was a really good sign. It meant that she was genuinely excited about it and thought it could work.

"Everyone is excited about it. Frankly, I think the staff is just as sick of Devon not working as she is."

"That's great news," Dad said.

"And it certainly doesn't hurt that the first model is someone they all know and love," Mom said, beaming at me. Even though I was anxious about the whole Devon-cutting-my-hair thing, it felt good to be doing something to make her proud for a change.

On Friday, I ran all the way from school to the salon. When I got there, I asked Megan if anyone had canceled on Rowan for early evening facials. I know the e-mails said there was no need to cancel, but I was a little worried that maybe one of them missed it and would call anyway.

She looked at the computer. "No. Should someone have?"

"No," I said, relieved. "Here's the rest of what I owe you." I gave her the rest of the money for the facials, and hoped it was all worth it.

As I swept, I kept my eyes on the front door so that I could pounce into action as soon as Kristen arrived for her four o'clock appointment. When the door chimed and she stood at the reception desk, looking a little tense around the mouth, I hustled up front to greet her.

"Hi there!" I said as if we were great friends and nothing at all was wrong.

"Hey, Mickey," she said. To Megan she said, "I won some drawing? I'm here for my facial."

"A salon drawing?" Megan said, checking some papers on her desk. "I haven't see—"

"Oh my gosh!" I said, cutting Megan off. "You won! Congratulations! Megan, I think the envelope that has Kristen Campbell's name on it is for her. Because she's Kristen Campbell. And she won! Yay!" I seriously needed to get a handle on my nervous ramblings. "I'll show her back, okay?"

Megan said, "I'm not asking a single question."

"I can't believe I won something," Kristen said. "I was looking for you at school to ask you about it, but I guess we kept missing each other. I don't even remember entering."

"Actually," I said, "Lizbeth entered you when she was in here last week."

"Oh," Kristen said. "Really?"

"Yeah."

I thought I saw her bottom lip quiver, like maybe she was about to cry, but she said, "If we were talking then I might tell her thank you."

"I'm sure you guys will talk again soon," I said.

"Don't count on it."

"In here," I said, showing her to the little room

with the tan curtain hanging between the two chairs. I showed her to the chair farthest from the door. She set her purse on the floor and took her seat.

"Rowan will be here in just a sec," I told her.

Kristen took a deep breath and leaned back in her chair. I quietly closed the door and breathed a sigh of relief that the plan was officially in action.

Lizbeth arrived at ten minutes after four. As I approached the front desk, she turned her eyes toward me and gave me a warm, friendly greeting.

Not really.

"Ugh," is what she actually said.

"Hi, Lizbeth," I said as I ignored yet another quizzical look from Megan. "I'll show her back," I told Megan. Then I turned back to Lizbeth. "Ready?"

"I didn't think you worked Fridays," Lizbeth said, her feet firmly planted.

I realized this was not going to be easy. Seeing Lizbeth's defiant stance there in the lobby made me realize I was crazier than even I thought. "Lizbeth, really, I'm so sorry for ever saying anything, even a single word, to Kristen. I didn't mean any harm by it."

Lizbeth tossed her long hair over her shoulder in that casual-but-not-really way.

"I was just trying to make conversation with her," I said. "How was I supposed to know it was a secret?"

"You shouldn't have been listening to us in the first place," Lizbeth said, looking down at her feet.

I knew she was right. "I'm sorry," I said again. "I really am."

Lizbeth finally looked at me straight on. "I'm just mad about the whole thing."

"Have you guys talked at all yet?"

She shook her head. "No. It's such a mess. I don't know what to say to her. I never told her I'd take her, but I always bring her to the country club parties. I don't blame her for being mad or hurt."

"Don't worry," I said. "I'm sure it'll all work out."

I motioned for Lizbeth to follow me to the back. For the plan to work I had to get her to speak freely, but at just the right time. And we only had seconds—as soon as Kristen heard Lizbeth's voice, she'd know it was her and would probably throw a fit.

Just as we got to the spa door, Lizbeth said, "Can I tell you something?"

"Sure," I said.

"It's just, I really want Kristen to go with me tomorrow night. I always did. Everything just got so messed up."

I opened the door for Lizbeth and showed her to her chair.

It was time.

I silently showed Lizbeth to the facial chair, and Rowan came around the curtain from Kristen and shot me a look. I put my finger to my lips, begging her to be quiet.

"Excuse me?" Rowan stage-whispered. An exaggerated sigh came from Kristen's side of the curtain, like she was totally being disturbed as she tried to Zen out.

"Sorry!" I begged. I gestured to Lizbeth, shrugging helplessly like it wasn't my fault that she was there early.

Rowan tapped her wrist where her watch would be. All facial appointments were to be made a half hour apart, and I'd purposely scheduled Lizbeth's appointment fifteen minutes early.

"Sorry," I mouthed and smiled meekly as if there was nothing I could do about it. Rowan shook her head, her mouth pulled tight. Thankfully, though, she went back to the other side of the curtain to continue working on Kristen.

I pulled up the small stool that was in the corner and sidled up next to Lizbeth, whose eyes were closed. "So," I said softly but right in her ear. Lizbeth pulled away from me. I turned around and grabbed two freshly sliced cucumbers from the tray and plopped them over her eyes. "Close your eyes and relax," I said.

CHAPTER 23

"You said you really wanted Kristen to go to the party, huh?" I whispered. Lizbeth twitched away from me, but then nodded her head.

"Well," I whispered. "Then why didn't you invite her?"

She shrugged her shoulders. I could tell she was starting to get a little creeped out by my behavior.

"You must know why. She's your best friend!"

Lizbeth snapped a cucumber off one eye and looked at me. "Shouldn't we be quiet?" She whispered, nodding toward the curtain and the mystery person on the other side.

"No, no," I said. "Just me. She"—I pointed toward the curtain—"won't mind *your* talking." Lizbeth seemed suspicious, but put the cucumber back over her eye. "So . . . what happened?"

"She's my best friend," Lizbeth said in a low voice,

but above a whisper. "I, like, love her like a sister. But she's so outgoing and fun and funny that when she's in a room no one notices anyone else within a five-mile radius."

I heard rustling on the other side of the curtain, and was sure that Kristen had not only heard Lizbeth, but probably already knew it was her. I tried to nudge her along more quickly by mmmhmming to her.

"The thing is," Lizbeth said, "I really like Matthew and I just know that once she gets around him and starts talking, he'll like her more than me. Two summers ago at camp there was this boy I told her I liked, and she said she'd go talk to him for me—you know, scope him out, see if he liked me. They started talking so much they forgot all about me. And Kristen was the one he ended up liking."

"I would never steal Matthew from you!" came a voice from the other side. Lizbeth lifted her head, cucumbers and all, and turned toward the voice. The curtain ripped open, and Kristen stood before us, her face green and tears in her eyes. "And you know I didn't mean for that to happen with what's-his-name at camp that one time!"

"Okay, that's it!" Rowan said, throwing her hands up in defeat. "I'm going outside. Let me know when you're done playing games."

Lizbeth finally took off her own cucumbers, and I

scooted back on the stool toward the corner of the tiny room, which was suddenly feeling suffocating.

"I know you didn't *mean* to," Lizbeth said. "That's not the point."

"Well, what *is* the point?"

"The point?! The point?!" Lizbeth was clearly on the verge of hyperventilating. I hoped she didn't pass out because I totally didn't know CPR. When she finally got the words out, I just wanted to tell her she was crazy. "The point is—you're prettier than me! And more fun! And everyone likes you more!"

Kristen and I both *pshaw*ed at the same time. Luckily they didn't seem to hear me.

"Not true!" Kristen said. "That's just . . . stupid!"

"Oh, thanks a lot."

"No, you know what I mean. Lizzie." She took a second to take a deep breath, stepping closer to Lizbeth in her chair. "I honestly don't know what I did to make you ditch me for the fund-raiser tomorrow night. I mean, I can't believe you'd think you'd *need* to ditch me. I didn't know I was such an awful friend."

"You're not! Seriously, K, you're not. It just seems like sometimes you don't really listen to me when I tell you I like someone. It's like you don't take me seriously or something, and then when that guy is around you say things that embarrass me and make me want to hide. Before I know it, he's looking at you and not me."

"Lizzie," Kristen said, tears forming in the ridges of the thick seafoam paste of the mask, "I didn't know. I didn't mean to. I'm so sorry! I feel awful!" The tears ran into her mask and she started to look like her face was melting.

"I know," Lizbeth said. "Maybe you could just, well, tone it down a bit? Let me be in the spotlight sometimes—or at least around guys I like?"

"Of course, totally, one hundred percent. I swear!"

They started hugging, and laughing then, as Kristen got facial mask goop on Lizbeth's shoulder. Lizbeth didn't care, though. "I'm sorry I didn't ask you before," Lizbeth said. "But do you want to go to the fund-raiser thing with me tomorrow night? I know it's short notice and all."

"Of course I'll go!" Kristen said. "Will you help me shop for a dress tomorrow?"

"Totally." Lizbeth smiled, and they hugged and cried a little more.

At some point during all their party talk, they finally remembered that someone else was in the tiny room with them. They turned their eyes on me; I nervously eyed the hot wax bowl that sat nearby, hoping they didn't decide to fling it at me as punishment for tricking them into talking.

"You," Lizbeth said, narrowing her eyes at me. I shrank back into the corner even more. "You promise to keep your mouth closed about everything?"

I pointed to my mouth. "I lost the key a long time ago."

"Good," Lizbeth said.

"And . . . well . . . y'know . . . thanks for staging this tearful reunion, Mick," said Kristen. Then she touched her cheek. "Oh gosh—my face is seriously starting to crack."

"I'll go get Rowan," I said, and left them alone to hug it out one last time in private.

CHAPTER 24

Before I left for work on Saturday, I sat in front of my vanity to say good-bye to my hair. I had cut out some styles from magazines the night before, but there was no telling what Devon would do once she had the scissors in her hand.

From the moment we opened our doors, the salon was slammed. It reminded me so much of my first day working at Hello, Gorgeous! except this time, I knew what I was doing.

Not only were we jam-packed with the regular weekend craziness, but it seemed like half the town needed us to get them ready for the country club party that night. Violet, Giancarlo, Piper, Mom, Karen, and Rowan were all booked solid with clients every second of the day.

And on top of all that, the big show was to start at two o'clock, and there wasn't an empty chair in the house.

The good thing about the salon being so busy was that I didn't have time to worry about how my cut would turn out. If I wasn't sweeping, I was showing clients back to the facials room or helping Gladys with the towels that were flying off the shelves or fetching drinks or doing any one of the hundreds of little jobs I was asked to do.

Time zipped by and before I knew it, Lizbeth and Kristen were in the salon with their moms to get their hair done for the fund-raiser. I waved to them, and Lizbeth motioned for me to come over.

"Hi, guys," I said, walking up to them, still a bit self-conscious of my plastic smock. I told myself that even if it wasn't glamorous, it was part of the job and the job was glamorous. It sort of helped.

"Hi," Lizbeth said. "We heard that there's going to be some demonstration here today on styling? That's so cool."

"Yep, it should be," I said.

"Is your mom doing it?"

"No. Actually, Devon is."

"Oh my gosh," Lizbeth said. "Seriously?"

I nodded yes.

"Why?" Kristen asked, confused. "Who's Devon?"

"That one," Lizbeth said, pointing to Devon, who had just come from the back. She looked extra

Devon-ish today, wearing a cherry-print black dress with a red corset belt.

"Oh," Kristen said. "Wait, isn't she the one that . . ."

"Yeah, isn't she?" Lizbeth said.

"No," I told them. "It was a misunderstanding. I'll tell you about it later."

"Who's she working on, anyway?" Kristen asked.

"That would be me."

"No. Seriously?" Lizbeth said.

"Serious as a military cut," I said.

Lizbeth laughed. "Why didn't you tell us?"

"You guys had a lot of stuff going on," I said.

"Mickey!" a voice called. I turned to see Devon waving me back. How could it be time already?

"Come with me," she said, guiding me away from Lizbeth and Kristen. They waved good-bye to me as if I were being marched off to the discount barber shop on the other side of town. I held the ends of my hair and said a silent good-bye to my long locks.

Devon had passed a message to me through Mom telling me not to wash my hair that morning. I figured it was because I'd get a good scrubbing at the salon, but when I leaned back in the sink Devon only got it wet.

"But I didn't wash my hair this morning," I said as she sat me up and put a warm towel on my head.

"Good. Just like I asked."

"But you didn't wash my hair just now!"

"Would you relax?" Devon said. "It's going to be fine."

Devon had me change into a robe, then met me in the break room. She didn't want to cut my hair in front of the audience. It was one thing to show clients how to style their own hair. But showing them how to cut? "That would be like a chef giving away his secret recipes," Devon explained.

Devon patted the chair that she'd set up for me. "Take a seat." I did as she told me. I would be courteous, obedient, and pleasant, the perfect customer. The last thing I wanted to do was, well, *anything* else that could provoke her to destroy my hair.

"Wait, my pictures," I said to Devon. "They're in my bag. I need to get them."

"What pictures?" she asked.

"Of what I want my hair to look like. I brought in samples, like you're supposed to."

"No way." She shook her head. "You said I could do anything I wanted with your hair."

"I did not!"

"You said you trusted me."

"I did?"

Devon turned her piercing green eyes on me. "Well,

you should. Come on, I have it all planned out in my head. You're going to look amazing when I'm done. Just go with it."

This was most certainly not the way a stylist was supposed to act with a client. They were supposed to consult first, talk about what kind of look the client wanted, then come to an agreement together. If Devon was so great, then why didn't she know all that?

"You're not supposed to do it like that," I said.

"Just trust me," she said for the second time.

And really, at that point, what other choice did I have?

One thing Devon was adamant about was not letting me see what my hair looked like until everything was done. I tried to figure out what she was doing as she snipped, clipped, and cut, but I couldn't get a good sense. The only thing I did know was that she gave me bangs. I could actually see the hairs hanging down in between my eyes. It was driving me crazy that I couldn't look at myself. "Can't I just have one quick peek?"

"Nope," she said. "You're just going to have to be patient. Now sweep this floor."

Okay, let me break it down. I knew I was working and all, but I was also part of the show—some might even argue the star. I must have made a pretty sour face becau—

"I'm joking!" she said, a smile cracking across her face. "Come on. Let's get out there and do this."

When I walked out on the floor, I was shocked to see how packed it was. I was so distracted, I even forgot to check myself out in the mirrors as Devon guided me to her station. There were two short rows of folding chairs filled with ladies and a couple of girls. The rest was standing room only. Women of all ages stood talking and waiting, and I noticed a couple of girls from my school and even . . .

Jonah! He stood right next to Eve. Had they come together? I'd try to get to the bottom of that later, but in the meantime I was just so happy that my friends were there for me on my big day.

Devon smiled as I sat down—facing away from the mirror—and whispered to me, "Don't worry, kid. It's going to be great."

I looked nervously at all the faces staring back at me. Lizbeth and Kristen, who smiled and waved looking faboosh with their country-club styles: Lizbeth's honey-colored hair in long, loose curls and Kristen in a double-plaited braid lying over her shoulder. Eve smiled and waved, too. And of course Jonah, who just shrugged like he wasn't sure how he'd gotten there.

Megan greeted a girl at reception. Her hair was pulled back in a messy ponytail, and she wore a fitted plaid button-down and worn-in jeans and, most importantly, a camera around her neck. Megan showed her over to Devon's station. I started to panic.

I motioned to Megan to come over to me.

"Who is that?" I whispered to her.

"A photographer from the *Rockland Register*. Isn't that amazing? They didn't send a reporter, but hopefully this girl will snap a few good pictures for the paper. We've never had press like this. Oh, look," she said, looking over her shoulder. "Here comes your mom. I guess it's time!"

When Mom saw me at Devon's station, she did a double take. "What?" I asked, my mind racing at what Devon might have done. She hadn't given me a mullet—I could tell that much—but the way Mom looked at me made me wonder.

"We're not letting her see until it's all over," Devon told Mom.

"Ah," she said. "Smart move, Devon. You two ready to get this started?"

No.

"Yes," we both said.

Mom turned to the gathered crowd and said, "Hello there! Thanks for joining us for our first in what we hope will be a series here at Hello, Gorgeous! I'm Chloe, owner of the salon, and we're happy to have this first demonstration of Be Gorgeous given by Devon, who is the newest member of our salon family. So, without further ado, I hand it over to you, Devon."

The crowd of ten thousand applauded, and I felt myself start to sweat. I didn't think so many people would actually show up, plus a news photographer, plus—were those cookies from CJ's that Megan was passing around? This had become a much bigger deal than I thought it would.

"Hi, everyone. I'm Devon, and I'm so happy you've joined us. If you like what you see here today and you want to come back and have me do your hair, just mention my demonstration and we'll give you ten percent off, okay? Now, this here is my model, Mickey," she said, clapping her hands on my shoulders, rather forcibly if I'm being honest. "We've already done the cut and have talked extensively about the styling problems she's having and what she'd like to be able to do with her hair. The solution I've come up with is simple." She opened one of her drawers and turned to face me with an electric razor. She flipped the switch and let it buzz and said, "Off with it!"

The crowd laughed; I did not.

"Just kidding," she said. She fanned my hair out over my shoulders and said, "Now, I have a theory that Mickey's hair is not unique. I bet there are many other heads of hair just like hers hiding under hats and scarves all over town, just begging for a way to look more glamorous and gorgeous. Today, I'm going to show you how to tame your frizzies with the best styling possible."

There, I thought. She'd said it, loud and without apology in front of the entire town—Mickey has frizzy hair! The worst kind of hair possible! Hearing someone finally admit to what I'd known all along made me somehow feel accepted, like my hair was just a different kind of normal.

"Most people don't think there's much you can do with this kind of hair," she continued. "But I'm going to show you some tricks to help tame it. And the first thing? Don't wash it every day."

I have to say, as someone whose mom owns a salon and sells a lot of product, that was a shocking thing to hear. Plus it seemed so dirty. What if my hair smelled?

"You don't want too much product on this kind of hair. Don't over-condition it, either. A little bit of relaxer is fine, but not too much."

Soon, Devon got to styling. I could feel that my hair had been trimmed, but it still hung long down my back. She mentioned that normally, split ends can also cause hair to frizz and that we should make sure we get a cut—at least a little trim—every six weeks to prevent split ends.

"Heat is its enemy, so it's important to towel dry the hair as much as possible before turning on the dryer. And it helps to think of the dryer as an iron gliding over the brush, which is like the ironing board."

"Now if you're asking me," Devon said, fanning my hair over my shoulders, "nothing else is needed. Doesn't she look gorgeous?" And to my surprise (and a little bit of embarrassment), everyone started clapping for me and my hair! Okay, they were probably clapping mostly for Devon's apparent wizardry, but it still felt good.

"If you want a little extra something," Devon said to me—and the audience, "we can accessorize as well. This will look adorable, I think." She took a pink, green, and white silk headband and tied it around my head. "You can fold thick headbands like this in half. That way, when you tie it at your neck it isn't so bulky. Also, to really keep it in place, you can add some bobby pins on the top and slide them under the first fold so they can't be seen. Voilà!"

When she was finally done, she spun me around to face the mirror and I couldn't believe what I saw: some girl with soft waves perfectly framing her face. My bangs lay gracefully across my forehead and made my eyes pop in a way I wouldn't have thought imaginable, and the back had a little bit more bounce to it.

I reached up to touch the hair to make sure it was really mine. It was. I couldn't believe it.

Mom stepped up to address the crowd and said, "Now I'm ashamed I never did this for my poor daughter myself. What's that they say about the shoemaker's children having holes in their shoes? Thank you, Devon!" Mom announced that Devon was currently taking new clients, and a rush of people went up to Megan's desk to schedule appointments.

"Mickey, your hair looks amazing!" Kristen said as she ran over to hug me.

Lizbeth followed her. "You were always gorgeous, but now your hair is killer," she said.

"Thanks, guys." I felt self-conscious about it, but still . . . I liked it. "Your hair looks really good, too. Both of you."

"Thanks," Lizbeth said. "Piper did an amazing job. But now if she's ever booked and I have a style emergency, I know I can go with Devon."

"You should," I said. "She's great. Obviously."

The photographer snapped a picture of me talking to the girls, and then she asked if she could get a shot of me and Devon. Once it was all done and the chairs had been put away, I finally had a chance to talk to Devon on my own. "Thanks, Devon. I love my hair. It looks amazing. And I'm so sorry for ever telling anyone you balded someone. Because you're a great stylist."

She smiled. "Thanks, Mickey. Make sure you tell your Mom that, too, okay?"

I put my smock back on, ready to finish out my day in the same old clothes but with gorgeous, flowing, bouncy hair. Mom was up front putting out some new products on the shelves—they'd sold a bunch when Devon made some recommendations. I stood next to her and said, "Well, what do you think?"

She put her hands on both my shoulders, turning me so that I faced her squarely. "I think you look gorgeous. But I've always thought you looked gorgeous. Did you really think your hair was so bad?"

I shrugged. "It's just that, your hair is perfect and straight and Dad's is perfect and wavy, and mine is this in-between mess that never looks right. I think it looks good today. And as soon as Devon sits me in front of a mirror and shows me how, I can probably make it look good tomorrow, too."

Mom smiled. And then, she did something she's never done in the salon before. She pulled me in for a hug. I wrapped my arms around her waist and she kissed my head. I didn't even worry about being embarrassed in front of Lizbeth and Kristen.

"Now get back to work," she said, patting me on the head.

Jonah and Eve stood in the lounge with Lizbeth and Kristen, who were about to leave with their moms.

They both looked so beautiful all glammed up and ready for a great night at the country club.

"Have fun tonight!" I said to Lizbeth and Kristen.

"Thanks!" Kristen said. "And thanks for everything you did for us, Mickey."

"You're welcome," I said, even though I didn't do anything but put things back the way they were supposed to be.

"Hey, we'll see you at school on Monday, right?" Lizbeth asked. "You'll sit with us at lunch?"

"Yeah," Kristen said. "You totally should. You, too, Eve. I don't know if you want to, Jonah, but you're welcome."

Jonah muttered something—he was probably in shock from being around so many girls—so Eve said, "No, Monday it's girls only. Maybe Tuesday. That cool, Goldman? Bring your friend Kyle."

Jonah's face turned a shade of red I hadn't seen since we had breath-holding contests as kids. He said something about "hanging with the boys" on Monday. "Well, have fun tonight," I said to Lizbeth and Kristen. "I want details on Monday!"

They laughed and said good-bye, and I hoped it meant we were all back on the road to becoming actual, real-life friends. "You really do look great, Mickey," Eve said. "But I've always been jealous of your hair."

"What? My hair? I'd kill to have your hair!" I told her.

"Mine? But it's just stick straight and blah. I wish I had volume like you do."

"Eve, that's probably the craziest thing I've heard all day," I said, and she laughed.

"Yeah, super crazy, Eve," Jonah said. "You look great . . . You're hot."

I had to replay that moment in my head before I could believe it actually happened. Did Jonah just say something nice to a girl? I could tell he had trouble believing it himself by the way he almost choked back that last word. Once everyone recovered from the shock he said, "Why don't you two just dig the hair you have? You *both* look good, okay? Now can I go? I think I'm starting to get hives from being here so long."

I wanted to come back to him with a crack about calling Eve pretty, but I couldn't do that when he had come there especially to see me.

"Why did you come, anyway, Jonah?" I asked. "I mean, don't get me wrong—I appreciate the support."

"She tricked me into it," he said, pointing at Eve.

"False," Eve said. "He was already on his way here when I ran into him."

"Well, I'm glad you came, Jonah," I said. "I know there's a million things you'd rather be doing."

He shrugged. "No biggie."

Once everyone had gone, I thought about how glad I was about the way things were going. I was so happy to finally have some new friends, but I was also aware of how lucky I was to have Jonah. Maybe I wasn't as into playing Warpath of Doom as I used to be, but he had always put up with my girly stuff, so I was happy to put up with his boy stuff.

For now, the most important thing was to learn to keep my mouth shut, to resist the urge to steal anything no matter how tiny, and to feel gorgeous—inside and out.

ABOUT THE AUTHOR

Taylor Morris is the author of several books including *Class Favorite* and *Total Knockout,* and her short stories and articles have appeared in *Girls' Life* magazine. She graduated from Emerson College in Boston, MA, and currently lives in New York City with her orchestra conductor husband. She does not get her hair cut in a fancy salon like Hello, Gorgeous! but she loves hearing from her readers about their latest hairstyles and favorite names for both real and imaginary nail polish colors. Visit her at www.taylormorris.com and tell her your favorites!

Photo by Silas Huff